I0543642

APOCALYPSE: DRAGONS!

JACQUELINE DRUGA

Copyright © Jacqueline Druga 2020

The moral rights of the author have been asserted.
All rights reserved. No part of this publication may be reproduced, stored in or introduced into a retrieval system or transmitted in any form or by any means, electronic, mechanical, photocopying, recording or otherwise without prior written permission from the publisher.

This novel is entirely a work of fiction. Names, characters, places and incidents are either the product of the author's imagination or are used fictitiously, and any resemblance to any person or persons, living or dead, is entirely coincidental. No affiliation is implied or intended to any organisation or recognisable body mentioned within.

Published by Level Up in the United Kingdom in 2020

Cover illustration by Sippakorn Upama
Cover by Claire Wood

ISBN: 978-1-83919-337-8

www.levelup.pub

For Miss Rita B, and all the help, support, suggestions and laughs you gave while I wrote this book.

ACKNOWLEDGEMENTS

A book is never truly written by one person when a support network exists. For that I'd like to thank Al, Paula and Connie for double- and triple-checking me.

My sons, Noah and Drew who really show what it means to love gaming and being brothers.

Rob and Sarah of Vulpine for always giving me the push and making me believe I am capable of trying anything.

And Conor of Level Up, for teaching, being patient and believing that we may have something here.

ONE

THE FAMILY

Ted knew women.

Not because he was some sort of Casanova but because he was surrounded by women ... always. That wasn't by choice.

He pulled into his parking spot behind his house after a strange day at work and saw the cars. All he could think to do was whine, maybe even hit his head against the steering wheel. Ted procrastinated going in.

My life sucks, he thought, *it really sucks.* He stared at the house.

There definitely was a group of chatty women in there. Really, he had no say so. While it was his home, it wasn't his house. It was a place to which he once vowed he would never return. Not that he hated it, he didn't. He just didn't think he'd be one of those thirty-something guys still living at home with his mother. Yet, a year earlier when his wife Gina took off with Ted's boss, he found himself back home and back in his room. A room that hadn't changed since Ted was a teenager. Other than being clean, it was exactly the same. Like some sort of weird memorial his mother kept of him … and he was still alive.

His mother was overprotective and over motherly to both Ted and his brother. More so recently toward Ted and he blamed himself for that. When Gina left him, Ted took a six month sabbatical from responsible life, during which he was stoned ninety percent of the time, and liked nothing more than to sit on the couch eating pizza and watching soap operas in between playing video games.

By the time he got himself back on track, his mother had settled into some sort of mama bear coddling mode with him, like he was eleven years old again.

Admittedly, Ted played that card, especially when his brother was around.

There was nothing wrong with his mother. She was a good woman, funny, outspoken and eccentric. Ted appreciated the fact she no longer cared if her hair was in style or not, if her makeup was too bold or mild. She was finally confident in herself and her only running complaint was her thickening midsection, which to his embarrassment she referred to as her never ending menopausal pregnancy.

His mom went back to school and got her degree in cosmetology and opened up a shop in the room behind the kitchen that was once a laundry room.

She built her business from a few clients to being a popular place to go. She was affordable in a neighborhood that had a lot of elderly folks and single parents. It wasn't a rich neighborhood, far from it. Ted knew his mom always looked forward to new clients so she could boast about her sons. How Ted was named after a rock star she had a drink with, while she was pregnant, during a layover in Buffalo. She claimed her oldest son, Lincoln, was destined for great things. Named after the car he was born in when she delivered during rush hour traffic, halting everything completely on the Fortieth Street bridge.

"Did I tell you my Lincoln is now manager of Arby's?" she'd tell people. "He brings in the big bucks now. Teddy? Oh, my Teddy is finding his way."

Every client. Every day.

Her shop, *Bea's Beauty Bundle* was the reason Ted delayed going in.

All the cars parked there meant it was Monday. Two-for-one 'tint and set' day. Which meant his Aunt Sally would be there too. He loved her but she was a bit much to handle. On tint and set days, Ted had to put on that polite, childhood front for the clients he saw.

It was time to go in. He grabbed the bag from the passenger seat.

He was hungry. Ted knew there'd be food in the fridge, at least some left-over takeout, which they always got on tint and set days.

He could have avoided the whole 'walking into his mom's home beauty shop' by simply following the path around the house to the front door. It was just a few extra steps, but the moment his mother realized he had arrived, she would do that, "Teddy, is that you? Come on in here, honey, and say hello."

As he made his way from the car to the little back yard, he saw one of his mother's clients, who just so happened to be his former high school Social Studies teacher. She was in her late eighties, and moved with a walker and the help of her senior citizen daughter.

"Is that you Teddy?" she asked.

His teacher and her daughter had almost the exact same hair. Gray strands that had been transformed into a really bright shade of light purple. Roller-set styles perfectly coifed into the classic Queen Elizabeth mode.

"Yes, Mrs. Feldman, it is me," Ted said.

"No Ted, 'it is I', not 'it is me.' You've gotten so big."

"I'm pretty old now, Mrs. Feldman."

"Teddy, I may not walk well but my mind still works. I'm not talking about your age, I'm talking about ..." she reached out and patted his small gut.

Ted sighed. "Soap operas, video games and pizza will do that."

"Or your mom's cooking."

"Hmm, yeah, well that too. Your hair looks great."

"Your mother and Sally are the queens of tint and set," Mrs. Feldman replied.

"You got the queen part down. Well, you have a good day. See you soon." Ted tapped her hand and walked to the back door. He could hear the hairdryers and smell the hairspray and perm solution. His mother seemed to be the only person in a thirty-mile radius that did perms. Especially those tiny little curl perms.

Who still requested them anyhow?

He walked in the back door. His mother was where she usually was: standing behind a client, her own hair especially big and blonde. She brushed solution on the foiled hair, all while dangling a cigarette from her mouth. How she hadn't caught a client or herself on fire yet, Ted didn't know.

"Teddy!" his mother spoke out cheerfully. "There you are."

"Hey, Ma."

"Ladies you know my Teddy?" she asked, taking the cigarette out of her mouth to flick the ash.

"Is this the one that works at Arby's?" a woman spoke loudly from under the dryer.

"Don't be ridiculous!" another replied just as loud. "Lincoln is the one that works at Arby's. He's a manager. Does that look like an Arby's manager's outfit?"

"It's not," Ted replied. "I work at the Exchange."

"The what?" the first woman asked.

The other woman repeated his answer. "The Exchange! They buy your old movies and music."

"Oh!" she waved out her hand. "I have stuff for you."

God help me, please. Let me get out of here. He thought. *My life so sucks.*

Aunt Sally sat sideways in the other barber chair, probably taking a break. She was a few years older than his mother, but her full face made her look at least a decade younger. Since her tailbone surgery, she had put on a significant amount of weight which made her irritated. It didn't help that she couldn't walk right, nor could she sit on her rear even three months after surgery. She did, however, get one of those vintage, vibrating belt machines off eBay for some evasive exercise. "Hey, Teddy," she said. "How was work?"

"Long, I actually spent four hours with one customer because he brought in every box from his grandfather's house. Oh! I did get you something."

"You thought of me?" Sally asked.

"Of course, as soon as I saw it." He handed the bag her way. "*Dynasty*, seasons one through five on VHS."

Sally gasped out loud with excitement. "The original series?"

"Yep."

She gratefully grabbed the bag. "Are you kidding me? Who would let these go? I just love me my Patrick Duffy."

"He was hot back then," Ted's mother commented.

"And on that note …" Ted waved his finger. "I'm gonna get something to eat." He walked to the kitchen, lifting his hand in a gesture of farewell.

He looked around, he didn't see any takeout bags or pizza boxes. He opened the fridge.

"Teddy!" his mother called. "There's a chicken sandwich in the microwave with some fries. We ordered too much."

"Okay, thanks, Ma."

Putting food in the microwave was a weird quirk of his mother's. She didn't want to put it in the fridge because it never tasted right reheated, and she didn't want to leave it out on the counter. So, she put it in the microwave to keep the flies away and temperature controlled … or so she said.

After grabbing a can of soda and bottle of ketchup, he reached for the sandwich and fries, then started to leave the kitchen.

"Teddy!" his mother called.

Ted stopped. "Yeah?"

"When you get a chance can you check to see what's happening with my computer in the loft."

"It's an attic."

"Yes," she said. "Can you check it? It seems slow."

"It was fine last night when me and Link were playing."

"Not that one. The one by the bookshelf."

"Uh, Ma," Ted cringed. "That's like from last century. Just toss it out."

"No, see if you can fix it," she said.

"I don't think anyone can."

"Teddy."

"I'm really not a computer expert."

"You're young," Her voice wasn't so loud. She came to the doorway between her shop and the kitchen. "On a baseline you know more about them than I do."

"I'll see what I can do. I want to eat first."

"Your brother is supposed to come over to pick up that soup in an hour, so, I can have him look if you don't want to."

"My brother is coming over to finish the game with me. But …Whatever, doesn't matter. I'm just gonna …" he held up his sandwich. "Eat."

"Go on."

He was actually glad to hear that his brother was coming over soon. They were the tag team extraordinaire in the game *Wind and War*, and they were so close to finishing a major quest line that had never been solved that Ted didn't want to wait until evening.

Until then, Ted would eat and watch the soaps he had recorded.

He sat center couch and placed his sandwich on the coffee table, opening up the wrapper as a plate. He aimed the remote; started the show; squirted some ketchup on the corner of the wrapper; and popped open his soda.

Mondays were always good. They were like season premieres in tiny portions every week.

Other than video games, much like his Aunt Sally, continuing stories were his guilty pleasure. His favorite was a rebirth of an old soap opera called *The Secret Storm*. Often, he found himself googling original storylines and looking up clips online.

Ted was engrossed. On the soap, closing arguments were given and the jury went out to deliberate the events of the previous week. Of course, they returned on Friday, and always the last scene of the episode ended with the foreman stating, "We the jury find the defendant ..."

It ended with a version of the Perry Mason suspenseful, musical tritone, dun-dun-dun.

He had to wait all weekend to hear the verdict and as usual they were now pissing around with other storylines before getting back to it.

It was going to be guilty, he just knew it. Or was it?

Myra was on trial for the murder of her fiancé's stepsister's lover. Clearly a jury with a half of brain would know that Myra lacked the strength to strangle him. She just couldn't disclose that her alibi was Ricardo, the catering manager, with whom she had an affair, and who was the secret father of her baby. Ted had long since figured out who the murderer really was and just waited for the show to catch up.

He was fast forwarding through commercials when he heard from all the voices in the shop the excited call of, "Lincoln!"

What? Ted thought. Already?

The women were giggly and Lincoln ate it up and played to it.

"Oh, Mrs. Lawrence, is that you?" Lincoln said. "I didn't recognize you with the new hair color. You look eight years younger."

"Thank you, Lincoln."

Eight years. Not ten or five ... eight.

"And for my favorite two ladies," Lincoln said. "Brought you beef and cheddars."

"Is my boy not sweet or what?" his mother said.

"You are so sweet and generous Lincoln," added Aunt Sally.

Ted snorted a quiet laugh, shaking his head. Generous? The sandwiches were on sale two for one. And no one called Ted generous over the *Dynasty* tapes, yet they were a real find.

He'd wait in the living room while Lincoln did his thing. Until then, Ted un-paused his show and turned up the volume.

TWO

CHOICE

It was time. It was the moment.

The verdict.

Lincoln turned off the television.

"What?" Ted stood. "Put that back on."

"Nope."

"Give me the remote." Ted held out his hand, walking to his brother.

"Nope. You're pathetic. You were so engrossed you didn't even see me take it."

"That's because they're about to read the verdict. Give it back."

"No."

"Whatever." Ted walked to the television. He looked on the left side, then the right. He ran his hand under it. "How the hell do you turn this thing on without a remote?"

"If you don't know, you don't deserve to have it on. And did you forget? The game?"

"No, I didn't forget. I just have two minutes."

11

"Dude, the game," Lincoln said.

"Dude, two minutes."

"No."

"Fine." Ted plopped down on the couch. "Can you at least change your shirt? You smell of fast food."

"You didn't smell it when I came in here and took the remote. At least I have a good secure job."

"I do, too," Ted argued. "Mine doesn't leave me smelling like fries."

"And mine doesn't have me coming home smelling like marijuana."

Ted snickered. "Marijuana."

"I have benefits," Lincoln said.

"Okay, valid point." Ted stood. "Let's play."

"Mom wants her computer looked at," Lincoln said. "Should we do that first?"

"No." Ted said. "I don't know the operating system. It's Windows Ninety-Eight or something. Maybe not that old, but it's old. Why does she need it anyhow? She has the good computer, laptop and tablet."

"She says there's stuff on there. I brought an external hard drive. Let's just see what we can do and dump her stuff on a drive."

"Can't we just say we did and leave it at that?" Ted asked.

"No, because it will still be slow, I can't lie to her, and if we don't fix it, Mom will keep sending me texts. She uses speech-to-text and Siri doesn't understand her Pittsburghese and everything she sends ends up inadvertently politically incorrect, racist, offensive or all three because she doesn't read them before she sends."

"What are you talking about?"

Lincoln handed Ted his phone. "Look at the text I got this afternoon. My assistant manager saw it."

Ted took the phone and read the text out loud, "I can taking my computer to some buyers, as it is passible fortune to fix the gay wonton dump soup." Ted raised an eyebrow. "What the hell?"

"Yeah exactly. It's all the time. If you read it out loud real fast you can figure it out."

"What's it supposed to say?" Ted asked.

"Read the next message? When I sent a 'what?' she sent the translation to me with a laughing face."

Ted read the next one. "Lincoln my computer has some virus, is it possible for you to fix it today when you come for the soup?" He returned the phone. "Wow, she was off."

"Yeah, I don't think it's a virus, just old. We'll run a scan while we play. Deal?"

Before he even muttered the word, 'Deal', Ted was on his way to the third floor.

<><><><><>

The door to the attic had a sign on it that read, 'Bea's Hive' with a little bumble bee on it. One of his mother's badly made attempts at home art décor. The attic was a decent size, finished, a few boxes of photos, craft stuff, a small bookshelf and old computer table pushed tight against the walls; for the most part it was a wide-open empty area. Not a stitch of furniture. Their mom liked to have the floor to work on. The good computer and computer table were set up in the alcove next to a large window that actually had a great view of the city in the distance.

All that space and she shoved it into the smallest area. But Ted could see why, the view alone was worth sitting there for. Although, when he used the computer for gaming, he never paid attention to the view.

Ted opened *Wind and War* and sat down. "Ready."

"Hold on," Lincoln turned on the old computer, "God, it takes forever to boot up."

"What does she use it for anyhow?" Ted asked.

"I don't know. She said she has emails on here from when emails first started."

"Do you think there's really anything wrong?" Ted questioned. "I mean, it could just be old."

"Maybe." Lincoln replied. "Who knows. Okay booted. Let me run the scan." His fingers clicked on the keyboard. "This will take longer than the game." After a hard, final strike of a key, he hurried over to join Ted on the other computer.

In one motion, he dropped into the chair and grabbed the control.

"You should have changed your shirt." Ted sniffed. "You smell like food."

"Shut up."

Ted laughed. "I'm still hungry."

"You're always hungry." Lincoln joked. "Wait. What the heck? Were you playing last night without me?"

"No. Why would I do that?"

"To gloat," Lincoln said. "If you didn't play, how did we get Meteor's Flaming Sword? We were still six basilisk eyes short for the hand in."

Ted grunted. "Mom. Bet she played it."

Lincoln nearly shrieked. "Why does she do that? Play her own game. Anyway, we need that sword."

Ted watched as his brother had first go of their shared avatar, fingers moving fast. They mocked the lame dialogue of the NPCs and goaded each other in between loud screaming and cheers.

Even though Ted was mad about his mother playing the game, the sword was pretty cool. Of course, her getting on the game came as no surprise, she did the same thing when they were little kids with *Guitar Hero*. She would wipe out all their high scores to be funny.

After an hour of gathering up the items they needed for the final hand in to spawn the boss of the mysterious quest they had discovered, they fell silent. It was Ted who had control of their warrior avatar when the kindly old lady for whom they had been performing chores transformed into a vast reptilian monster filling the screen, roaring at them with a mouth full of sword-sharp teeth.

"Jeez," muttered Lincoln, "that's the last time I help ol' grandma."

A toe-to-toe fight was impossible. But the flaming sword gave Ted the option of running while casting blasts of fire as rapidly as the timer allowed. It took maybe ten minutes, he wasn't counting, but Ted eventually wore the monster down. When it died, Lincoln, who had been wise enough to can the smart remarks while Ted was concentrating, leapt up and they joined together in shrieks of happiness and a high five.

"Dude, did you see that, it was so sweet," Ted said excitedly. "The way …"

"I know. It was …" Lincoln shifted his eyes to the computer screen, his demeanor totally changing to one of confusion. "What the heck?"

In the midst of their post-game celebration, the screen changed.

"Ted what is this?" Lincoln asked. "This is so weird."

The screen looked like a landing page of a website. A surreal painting of a blue and pink sky, mountain range in the back, and in the center was a woman who looked like a floating angel. A small square was across her feet.

"Was this supposed to happen?" Lincoln asked. "Did you hit any buttons?"

"No, I didn't hit anything."

The angel woman floated happily, then behind her small specks of black flying creatures appeared in the background. They

16

grew larger and larger until it became clearly recognizable that they were dragons. The one dragon swooped close behind her, swinging around in front until its face was the whole screen. It roared, releasing fire that simulated burning the entire image. After everything went back, the sequence started again.

"Dude, you know what this is?" Ted asked. "It's a…" He snapped his fingers several times, then pointed. "It's an instanced dungeon. Dude, we won this. This … this is our reward. It's a unique adventure or zone or something. That square is probably the enter button. We should click on it."

"You think?"

"Yeah," Ted replied without hesitation.

With single, dramatic, hard tap of his finger, Lincoln clicked enter.

The sound of thunder and lightning played through the cheap speakers, then it went silent and the screen became black. Chinese symbols were written on the screen with the English translation beneath, 'Thank you for being the first to play'.

Both brothers cheered loudly.

"First to play!" Ted shouted. "Ever. I mean out of everyone, we're the first. How freaking cool is that?"

"Mom still got us the sword."

"Oh, who cares we have …"

The words disappeared. No more sounds. Nothing.

"What?" Ted blasted.

"Aw," Lincoln groaned out. "Come on. Seriously."

"Is the computer dead?' Ted asked and sat back down

"No."

"This sucks. Try hitting escape."

Lincoln reached down for the keyboard when it happened.

A slight rumbling began causing the pane of glass on the window to make a vibrating sound. A noise that sounded like a muffled train grew louder and louder. Just as both brothers turned their attention to the window, the large black and dark-green body of a beast flew by.

What was it?

It didn't take long to get their answer.

After the creature made its close pass by the window, it then flew a bit farther out as if it were circling and it came more fully into view. The wingspan was huge and the tail long. The mythical creature extended its neck as it aimed to fly upward. It widened its vicious looking mouth and released a roaring 'caw' just before it shot a blazing inferno of fire upward.

Both Ted and Lincoln reacted the same way, at the same time.

Both of them screamed a single 'uh' as they hurried to stand. Lincoln stumbled back knocking the chair over.

"What the, what the …?" Lincoln could barely speak.

The words flowed fast from Ted, "That wasn't us? Right? It's not us."

"No! That can't be. Jesus, Ted. We have to get mom and get her out. Aliens or something arrived."

"Dude, that was a dragon."

"Aliens."

With no time to argue, Ted spun around, away from the window and stopped cold.

There in the center of the open area of the attic was a man. A tall elderly looking man. His hair was white and long, as was his beard. He wore a long, purple, shiny robe and carried a staff. The hat on his head looked like it was supposed to be a cone but it had gone limp and looked just as grumpy as the man himself.

The strange instant visitor shook his head. "What have you two done?"

THREE

REALITY

Hallucinogens taken in his youth were coming back some way or somehow, or some really screwed up stuff was happening, either way, Ted bolted down the stairs, his brother close behind. They ran from the third floor, to the second to the first, nonstop.

"Mom!" Ted called out. "Mom!"

"Mom!"

Ted stopped in the hallway on the first floor. "Okay, hold on. We sound insane."

"I know what we saw."

"I know."

"Ted, there is some strange dressed guy on the third floor, who came out of nowhere."

"Or did he?" Ted asked. "If the ground shook down here and those things …"

"Aliens."

"Dragons," Ted said.

"Whatever."

"My point, Lincoln, if they were screeching and blowing fire, wouldn't mom be yelling for us?"

"No. Mom probably didn't hear a thing over the dryers."

"Okay. True. But let's go calmly and talk to her."

Still hyped up, they walked down the short hall, through the kitchen into the shop. Their mom was styling a woman's hair, teasing it, spraying it and curling it. One customer sat under the dryer, and Aunt Sally was doing nails.

They were acting normally.

Sally looked at them. "Everything okay? You two look like you saw a ghost."

Lincoln stepped forward. "Did you guys feel that a minute ago?"

"Feel what?" Sally asked.

"Like a rumbling, earthquake," Lincoln said. "Giant truck going by."

Sally shook her head. "We didn't feel anything. I didn't. Bea?"

Bea shook her head. "No, nothing. Did something happen?"

"So," Ted said. "You didn't feel the ground move or, say, hear some monster sounding thing."

Bea stopped styling the customer. "I'm sorry, did I hear what?"

"Mon ... ster," Ted replied with a stammer. "Like a growl or roar."

They all just started at them.

"Boys," Bea said. "You been smoking that wacky tobaccy?"

Ted shook his head and immediately walked to the door and out. Lincoln followed right behind.

He looked to the sky, nothing. The man across the alley was working on his car. A kid road down the street on a bike. Kids laughing and playing were the only noises in the distance.

Surely, if there were something like a dragon or alien flying overhead, things wouldn't be so calm.

"What the hell?" Lincoln asked.

"None of it was real?" Ted asked. "It seemed so real. How can we both imagine the same thing?"

"If none of that was real, does that mean ..." Lincoln nodded at the house. "The strange man in the attic wasn't real?"

Ted didn't reply. He, like Lincoln, looked up to the third floor and then they both just raced back in the house.

<><><><>

The strange man in the purple robe sat on the computer chair in the center of the empty attic.

"He's real," said Lincoln.

"I see that." Ted stepped into the room.

The man looked bored, sitting there, holding his staff, with legs crossed.

"I must say," he spoke. "It is most ingenious to put mobility to your chair. I do, however, find your furnishings quite meager. Do you live in such squalor and destitution that you cannot afford anything more than a moveable chair in your cottage?"

Ted moved his hand around as he spoke. "This is just one room of many. There is furniture elsewhere."

"Who are you?" Lincoln asked.

"I am Samuelson, the all-powerful and all-knowing Wizard of Aberly." He nodded, but he didn't seem too impressed with himself, speaking almost in an annoyed, deadpan manner.

"Samuelson, the Wizard. What … what are you doing here?" Lincoln asked.

"I have no doubt the Maniacal Master had something to do with my arrival. He probably handed you the key and you opened the door."

Ted shook his head. "I'm confused. The Maniacal Master?"

"You have not heard of him in your world?"

"No," Ted replied. "We have several people who could be called 'maniacal', but no one that goes by that name. Maybe he's just popular in your world, and what world, you know, would that be?"

"Your world."

"No," Ted said. "Your world."

"My world is your world. Do you think I have come from the stars?"

Lincoln shrugged. "Or maybe another realm?"

"Preposterous. There is only one realm. We share the same world just different times. While you were doing whatever it was you were doing in your vacant cottage, I and my band of heroes were deep on a quest to destroy the Master and all he created that causes destruction."

"And … and … What would they be?" Lincoln asked.

"Draconem, fire breathing destructive creatures."

"Dragons," Ted said with an arrogant nod. "I told you."

"And they should not be taken lightly," Samuelson said. "We have been in pursuit of them. They have burned not only our villages but also our land. If we were not to stop them, they would destroy everything. They appeared shortly after the Maniacal Master made his presence known. He resides and hides in a distant lair drawing power from a dark force. We were fighting the draconem and searching for him when we were pulled into a hole in the sky."

"So, let me get this straight," Ted held up his hand. "Some guy has created all this death and destruction in your world, and some sort of portal opened up and you were sucked right through?"

Samuelson nodded. "Slow but wise you are. That is what happened. Because of my abilities I was drawn to the source of the beings who opened the portal. You."

Ted and Lincoln both looked at each other. "The game."

"How is that even possible?" Lincoln asked.

"Obviously this Maniacal Master has some sort of power and locked into our prize game. It doesn't matter if it sounds feasible or not: it's happening, look at this guy."

"Unfortunately, it is all not so simple," said Samuelson. "I am not the only one that arrived. Just the only one who came to the source. My band of heroes passed through as well. They are out there. We must find them. They will be lost and confused. Unlike I, who art all-knowing and all-powerful."

"Obviously not as powerful as the Maniacal Master," Ted said, then he had a thought, a way to test Samuelson. "Maybe you can tell me what happened with the trial I was watching on *Secret Storm*."

"If you must know …"

"Holy shit stop," Ted halted him. "Do you know?"

"I am all-knowing and powerful."

"Then don't tell me. I want to watch it," said Ted.

"Wait," Lincoln said. "If you came through, along with your heroes and the Draconem, that means …"

"Yes," Samuelson replied. "The Maniacal Master has descended on your world as well. He will not be kind, you must know. For many will die. Two thirds of the land will perish in his pursuit of destruction."

"What do we do?" Ted asked.

"You must help me find the other heroes."

"Who are?" Lincoln asked.

"The Slayer, the Barbarian, the Prince and the Fairy."

"Oh my God," said Lincoln. "This isn't real. It can't be. It sounds like a book or movie, or even a game. Dragons, a Wizard,

Slayer, Barbarian, Prince and Fairy, along with a," Lincoln brought his fingers up to form quotes. "Super bad guy."

"Did you just do air quotes?" Ted asked.

"I did."

"Enough," Samuelson said annoyed. "The banter is tiresome. You brought us here, you need to bring us back together and then you both shall join us in the quest to defeat the Maniacal Master and stop the draconem from destroying all."

"Yeah." Ted nodded. "I'm not super concerned about the dragons. I mean, yes, they're destructive, but if they're flying about out there, we have some pretty decent weapons that will take them down. A missile fired from a fighter jet. We're good."

"Believe what you believe," Samuelson said. "I know what needs to be done. It is your responsibility. This lies upon your shoulders. Because it was you who opened the portal, it is only you two who can close it."

"How do we do that?" Ted asked.

"Quickly. While you cannot see it or hear the cries of your people just yet, the destruction has begun. Find the lair of the Maniacal Master, stop the source of the power, or kill the Maniacal Master or both," Samuelson replied. "Preferably both."

"Can we?" Lincoln asked.

"It is not a matter of what you can do, it is a matter of what you must do. On this ..." Samuelson said. "You don't have a choice."

<><><><>

Directly after Samuelson gave his instructional speech, Lincoln left. He went home as if everything was all well and fine and he was just going to mull it over. The fact that he didn't stay to brainstorm irritated Ted, but not as much as the current endeavor. He sat at the dining room table, phone in one hand, scrolling with thumb, as he propped his face in the palm of his other hand, trying not to look defeated.

"Oh, come on. Really?" Ted groaned and grunted. "What the hell. No."

"Teddy, honey," his mother said. "You're not eating. Your grilled cheese will get chewy and tomato soup will get cold. What in the world has you so engrossed?"

"*Edge of Night.*"

"The old soap opera?" she asked.

"Yeah, they took it down. I was watching the old episodes faithfully, and they took it down." His hand came to the table in frustration, nearly hitting the tray style plate that had his sandwich neatly cut in a triangle and bowl of soup. "Now, I am just left hanging. Nicole was on trial, and Debbie just started talking again, she's the only one that can clear Nicole's name and … they took it off."

Samuelson who sat at the other end of the table, spoke up, "Adam Drake put her on the stand and she pointed to Pamela."

"Oh," Ted said with relief. "Thank you. That's what I was hoping would happen."

"Try old episodes of *Another World*," Samuelson said. "It's a good one."

"Look at you," Bea waved out her hand. "You are living up to that name all-knowing. How do you like your grilled cheese and tomato soup, Mr. Wizard?"

"This is the most delicious meal I have ever encountered. To think a woman of your beauty and talents dwells in a home without a lover."

"Hey, now," Ted looked up from his phone. "That's my mom."

"Is she not still a woman?"

"Guy, stop, okay?" Ted cringed.

"So sweet," Bea tapped him on the shoulder. "You boys have a good night; I'm going to bingo." She walked to Ted and kissed him on the cheek.

"Ma, Bingo? Right now? With all that's going on? I showed you the news story: they spotted dragons."

"It's not real Teddy, it's a hoax. Look it up. I did. People photoshop dragons into pictures all the time. And if it is true, they're in the mountains, that is not near us. For now, I am going to bingo."

"You're as bad as Lincoln was for leaving," Ted commented.

"Your brother has to work. Not everyone like you has Tuesday and Wednesday as their weekend. I'm out. Mr. Wizard you make yourself at home here."

"I shall."

"And I hope you have good luck finding your party. Check the world wide web, you never know."

Ted mumbled, "Finding your party." He looked up at Samuelson. "How do you know all this stuff? And don't say you're all-knowing. Because if you were you'd know where to find the puppet, pauper, pirate, poet, pawn and king."

"It's the Prince. And how do you know the words to such an old song?"

"How do *you* know they are the words to such an old song?"

"I'm all-knowing."

"Ha!" Ted laughed. "Selective all-knowing."

"True. I am all-knowing on things the universe wants me to be knowing of. And, it's a stock phrase, which I use when I actually am in the knowhow. So tell me, how can this world wide web help?"

"First of all, only old people and computer illiterates call it that," Ted placed down the phone. "Second, it can help if let's say, the 'Fairy' was flying around a convenience store and then the post went viral, other than that, it's useless in helping find a motley crew that just arrived a couple hours ago."

"Ah, we don't know that. And are you going to finish your meal? I am famished."

"Help yourself." Ted pushed his plate forward. "What do you mean?"

"I arrived a couple of hours ago; we come from the same realm, only a different time, when we came through the portal, I arrived at you and your brother, the source," Samuelson said. "The others could have arrived a day or two ago or it might even be tomorrow."

"What's the uh … time difference? I mean, how far back could they have arrived?" Ted asked.

"No more than several days, I would think."

"That does help. But … let me just ask one more thing. You said we're from the same realm. I don't ever remember a time in history when dragons weren't a myth."

"Prior to the arrival of the Maniacal Master, I did not think they were more than a myth myself."

"Do you think he brought them or created them?" Ted asked.

"All I know is we can slay them, but more will appear until we stop him. They are manifestations from the mind of the Maniacal Master."

Ted bobbed his head. "Good to know." He lifted his phone again. He could very easily search for news stories or posts about a potential fairy or someone claiming to be a prince, and Ted would, that is, after he had exhausted his search for old episodes of *Edge of Night*.

FOUR

DONATIONS

"Thank you for choosing Arby's," the pleasant young girl behind the counter said. "What can I get for you today?"

"Hi," Ted replied. "I'm looking for my brother Lincoln."

"Oh, Link, sure hold on." She slipped from behind the register and went into the back.

Lincoln came to the front. "Ted, what are you doing here?"

"I'm here asking the same question. What are you doing?"

"Um ... working and it's almost the lunch rush."

"Yeah, well we have a bunch of people to find. And did you see the news? They reported dragon sightings again. It's happening and it's real."

"Have they started burning things?" Lincoln asked.

"Not ... not yet. But they will."

"We can't do anything about that, Ted," Lincoln argued. "And I can't leave. For some reason we're dragged into this but I have a job. If you don't get to yours then you won't have one."

"I'm off today."

31

"Good, then you can search for the missing portal people until I'm done working. And … where … where is the Wizard?"

"I left him at the house," Ted said.

"With Mom?"

"Well, yeah, I mean, he won't get out of that robe; I'm not bringing him out in public"

"Can't say that I blame you." Lincoln looked around. "Look I'll cut out after the lunch rush. We'll go grab the Wizard and start looking."

"Okay, I'll wait for you."

"That's two hours."

Ted shrugged. "I'm hungry and mom and Aunt Sally can watch the Wizard."

"You think that's wise?"

"What are they gonna do, feed and perm him to death?" Ted snorted a laugh. "So, I'll wait. Then we'll go."

"I don't know where we are even going to begin to look."

"I do," Ted said. "Last night, Samuelson told me that the others could have arrived days before him. Some screwed up time in the portal stuff. So, after I finished searching for archive episodes on *Edge of Night* …"

"The old soap opera?" Lincoln asked.

"Yes."

"Why?"

"Because I didn't finish a story line and they took them offline."

"That's a sickness bro."

"Whatever, as I was saying … I started looking up posts on social media. Maybe people seeing weird stuff, news stories."

"What keywords did you use."

"Swords, dragons, weird people, stuff like that."

"And?" Lincoln asked.

"I think… I think I found something." Ted handed him the phone. "Read that."

Lincoln exhaled, annoyed, cast his eyes upon the phone and his whole expression changed as he read the headline. "Street performer wows crowd with flaming swords as she reenacts *Game of Thrones*."

"Yep." Ted nodded proudly. "That has to be one of them. Look at the picture. Unless you're in Vegas, no one gets that much into costume."

"She's hot," Lincoln said.

"Yeah, I know."

"I think it'll be cool if she is one of the hero team. Just sayin'"

"Me, too, dude."

"Which one do you think it is?" Lincoln asked.

"If I'm correct. This …" Ted said. "Is the Slayer."

<><><><>

The radio DJ's thought they were witty, talking about the dragon situation, as if really, the world needed them.

They started discussing the situation just as Ted and Lincoln sat outside their mother's house before going in.

The DJ's traded blurbs back and forth.

"And now," the one DJ said. "They're saying there are three ... three dragons flying over Butler Knob. Which is north of Breezewood."

The other DJ immaturely hyena laughed. "Three not four or two."

"Three. You know there is a military base out there. Bet they are trying some sort of new plane."

"I think this all a hoax. Have you seen the pictures? Photoshop."

"Without a doubt."

"Dragons in the twenty-first century ... um, yeah."

"Speaking of dragons, sending this out to all those listeners who are enjoying this last viral news ..."

And then the song, 'Puff the Magic Dragon' began to play.

"Jesus." Lincoln shut off the radio. "Okay, let's go grab him ... but after we look for this Slayer, we get my car from Arby's. I love gaming, but this is beyond that and I am not going to be trapped into making this my life's mission."

"We may not have a choice. We are responsible."

"If it wasn't us, it would be someone else," Lincoln said.

"Oh my God, you sound exactly like Felicia when Mac told her she was responsible for the actions ..."

"Stop. Who?" Lincoln asked.

"Felicia Gallant and Mac Cory."

"Do we know them, are they clients of mom's?"

"No, they were on *Another World*. There's a channel dedicated to old soaps and—"

"You're ridiculous." Lincoln opened the door to the car, holding the takeout fast-food bag. "At least there aren't a million cars here today." He walked up the path to the back door.

"It's not tint and set day."

Lincoln sniffed. "I still smell perm."

"Her clients are all over seventy, they think perms are still the rage." Ted opened the door.

"Teddy!" his mother said brightly, as she cut a woman's hair.

"Am I invisible?" Lincoln asked.

"Oh, honey I'm sorry. I couldn't see you around your brother."

"Ha!" Lincoln laughed. "I keep telling him he got fat." He kissed his mother on the cheek then set the bag next to Sally who was doing nails.

"You're home early," Sally told him. "And thank you. Did you bring the triple threat sauce?"

"In the bag," he replied. "By the way, where's our friend?"

"Oh," their mom replied. "Mr. Wizard is in the living room simply mesmerized by the television. I don't get it."

"I do," said Lincoln.

Ted tapped Lincoln on the shoulder. "I'll go get him."

"Thanks." Lincoln looked over to Aunt Sally who reached in the bag. "Are you checking for the sauce? I told you ..." he stopped when he heard the loudest scream of shock come from the living room.

Ted's 'Uh' was louder than the time he stepped in horse manure when they were posing for their cousin's wedding.

"Mom!" Ted yelled.

Lincoln raced in the room, as soon as he stepped in, unintentionally, he repeated his brother's reaction. "Uh!"

Bea came racing in the room. "What are you boys yelling about."

"What …" Ted pointed to Samuelson. "What did you do to him?"

"Oh," Bea waved out her hand. "We were slow, I gave him a little make over."

"Mom, you can't give a wizard a makeover," Ted argued.

"What … and just why not?" She laughed. "The Wizard family men can't have makeovers?" she fluttered her lips. "A haircut and shave. What's the big deal? He wanted it."

Ted grunted in frustration. "He looks like Sam Elliott from the movie *Roadhouse*, but with really white hair."

"Oh, that yeah, he didn't want much taken off and I had to give him a perm for a lift."

"I told you," Sally said. "I told you he looks too much like Sam Elliott. We all know your obsession with Sam Elliott, Bea."

"As opposed to making him look like Patrick Duffy."

"Ya managed both!" Ted shouted. "He's wearing the same thing Patrick Duffy wore in *Dynasty*. Could we have at least kept him in this century?"

Lincoln brought his hand to his own face, drawing his fingers slowly across his lips. "What happened to his clothes?"

"In the washer now, Bea answered. "He shouldn't wear them in public. I mean, you know how people get when they see for-eigners wearing the clothing of their land."

"Mom," Lincoln held up his hand. "There was so much wrong in what you just said, I'm going to ignore that."

"What?" she asked. "What did I say? Sally? Was I wrong?"

"I think he looks good. And wants to be called Sam now." Sally replied.

"I wonder why?" Ted tossed up his hands. "He's unrecogniza-ble. This isn't going to help when we look for the other members of his party."

"Tell me about it." Lincoln looked at Samuelson sitting on the couch with his shoulder length wavy, layered cut hair, blue plaid shirt and acid washed jeans. It was then he realized through the entire living room discussion about his makeover, that he never said a word. In fact, he sat there. Hand on one knee, staff in the other staring. "Is … he …alive."

"Sure he is," Bea replied. "He's just watching television."

"Mom, you probably killed him with perm solution," Ted said, then stepped closer to him and snapped his finger. "Samuelson,

Samuelson." No reaction. "Wizard! Hey Samuelson!" Ted raised his voice to a near scream. "Sam!"

With a slightly startled, 'huh', Samuelson turned his head and looked at Ted. "My apologies. Did you say something? I was watching the vividly colored show of yours, *Secret Storm*. It is so engrossing."

"Oh, yeah?" Ted asked with a different tone, then walked to the couch. "What's going on?" Just as he began to sit, Lincoln stopped him.

"No. We're going." He grabbed Ted's arm. "Sam ... as you want to be called now. Grab your staff. We think we found one of your team."

"That is wonderful." Samuelson stood. "Let us retrieve who-ever it is then."

Both brothers, along with Samuelson walked across the living room.

"Wait," Bea called out. "Since you're finding your friend, I as-sume they will be coming here. Should I take more chicken from the freezer?"

"Ah, poultry." Samuelson reached out to her. "A delicacy pre-pared by a woman embedded in my heart."

"Alright, let's go Tom Selleck," Lincoln said, giving him a tug.

"I thought I was Sam."

With no more being said, and before their mother could inter-fere any further, they led their re-imaged new friend out of the house.

Ted pulled into the parking spot and put the car in park. "Twenty dollars for parking."

"We're downtown. If we would have been here ten minutes sooner we would have had hourly rates."

"Not my fault…" Ted pointed to the back seat. "We had to chase him when he got out of the car at the first light and started screaming."

"Was pretty funny though," Lincoln said. "Especially when he started saying it was possessed."

"If you two are done playing tiddle me this," said Samuelson. "I cannot get out."

"Childproof locks, Guy." Ted opened his own door. "Can't take a chance."

Lincoln exited the car and opened the back door.

"Thank you," Samuelson said. "I must say for as frightening as this was at first, my appreciation has grown and this will be a re-markable battle vehicle."

"What do I keep saying?" Ted asked. "I don't worry about the dragons. With our military, those three will be shot down and it will all be over with."

"Hmm," grumbled Samuelson. "Have you not realized he will only create more?'

"What?" Ted asked. "What is this Maniacal guy? Like a God?"

"Or Worse," Samuelson replied. "Some say he is the devil himself."

"Well I don't buy it," Lincoln said. "There has to be a logical explanation. Let's just hope we find the Slayer."

"Where will we be searching?" Samuelson asked.

"Some place she was yesterday and the day before," said Lincoln. "Let's hope she's the right person."

<><><><>

Any doubt that the woman on the street corner wasn't the Slayer was tossed out the moment, they were close enough to hear her voice.

A small crowd had gathered around the woman, slightly blocking her from view.

"It is my greatest honor to take on this most precarious quest," she said boldly and loud. "It is but I who possess the power to slay what will besiege this land."

The Slayer wore tight, handmade leather pants. A partial suit of armor covered her chest and shoulders, and her arms were covered in the same material as her legs. Her hair was long, part of it was pulled into a ponytail while the rest was wild and full. She was tall and slightly muscular, her outfit seemed to highlight every curve and ripple of a muscle. She moved left and right, raising her swords as she spoke, as if she did some well choreographed dance.

Someone, and Ted assumed it wasn't the Slayer, had placed an empty Kentucky Fried Chicken bucket in front of her and clearly there was money in there.

"Is that her?" Ted asked.

Samuelson nodded. "It is she."

"Dude." Ted turned to Lincoln. "She's so hanging out with us."

"Fear not, my friends!" Slayer said dramatically. "For I am here. When the beasts fly from the sky, releasing their fiery wrath upon your villages, threatening to scorch your children, I will defeat them. I am the slayer of all draconem."

More people reached forward dropping money in the bucket.

"Who ... will join me in this battle which calls for only the bravest of souls to embark?" Suddenly her swords ignited. Blue and red flames shot upward; it was a medieval version of a Star Wars Lightsaber, only when they lit up, epic fanfare music seemed to come out of thin air.

"What the hell?" Lincoln looked up. "She has theme music?"

"Cool," Ted whispered.

"Does that happen all the time?" Lincoln asked. "Because it will be tough to pull a sneak attack."

"Only when she wants to announce her presence."

The crowd erupted in cheers and when they did, the 'blip-blip' of the police sired rang out.

"Shit," said Lincoln.

"What a beautiful machine," Samuelson said in wonder. "With the colorful flashing lights."

"Okay, alright," the police officer spoke. "Break it up. Everyone disperse." He made his way to the Slayer. "Miss, what did I tell you yesterday?"

"You have not joined my quest."

"As much as I would like to, I can't," the officer told him. "And you cannot do this without a permit. You can't panhandle around here, pretending you're Kahleesi, the mother of dragons."

"But I am not the mother of draconem. I am the Slayer of draconem."

"Yeah, but …"

"Does this womb appear to be one of which that would spawn eggs of a draconem?"

"Forget what I said about being the mother of dragons."

"I shall try," she replied.

"Look, I wouldn't be so hard-core about this, but you also can't be wielding weapons in the middle of downtown. It's dangerous."

"But I must prepare for the battle ahead. It is coming. You will thank me one day."

"I'm sure," the officer reached down for the bucket. "Looks like a lot of people are funding it."

"Sir, I do not need nor ask for reward. Take it for your good service."

"Are you trying to bribe me?"

"Okay, shit." Lincoln turned to Samuelson. "What is her name?"

"Basalous."

Lincoln cringed. "Okay, that's not gonna work." Lincoln stepped forward. "Basa! Basa. Oh my God there you are."

The officer turned around. "You know this girl?"

"Yes, yes, we do," Lincoln said. "It's our cousin Basa, we've been looking for her for days."

"She's, uh," Ted whispered. "Off her meds."

The officer nodded knowingly.

The Slayer balked. "I do not know these heathens. Weak men in strange clothing." She leaned toward Lincoln. "And one smells strange."

"Ha!" Ted pointed. "I told you. Even the chick gets it."

"Chick?" Basa asked. "Do I look like I spawn feathers? What lord has tasked you strange men to take me from my task?"

"Look, you don't know us..." Ted pointed. "Bet you know him." He dropped his voice to a whisper again to the police officer. "Her dad."

Slayer lowered his swords with a gasping 'Ah', she bowed to Samuelson. "Oh, you have found me. I thank you. But what ..." she stood upright, "has this world done to your appearance?"

The officer looked at Samuelson. "Anyone ever tell you that you look exactly like Sam Elliott in *Roadhouse*?"

"Yes, and my name is Sam."

The officer whistled. "Spitting image. Unreal. Okay ... get her home, back on her meds and please, don't let her do this again. I can't keep letting her go."

Ted stepped forward. "Thank you, officer." He looked at the name tag. "Bill Smith."

"Officer Bill Smith!" Slayer yelled. "Finally, I have been given your name. We will engage soon Officer Bill Smith."

"My girlfriend may not like that," the officer said.

"Find me when you are ready to battle the beasts. Their arrival is imminent."

Lincoln, inched the Slayer away, mouthing the words, 'thank you' to the officer.

The Slayer pulled her arm from Lincoln. "I am not of the drink. Nor am I a possession you snatch from a brothel. I can move on my own. Wizard, have you located the others?"

"No, not yet," Samuelson replied. "But we will. Soon. They are here somewhere."

"Wait," Ted said. "Hold on."

"What?" Lincoln asked.

Ted ran back the fifteen feet and grabbed the money filled bucket container from KFC, He clutched it close to his chest as he walked fast. "Just … you know, parking is expensive and uh …" he grabbed bills as he walked, shoving them in his pocket. "Battle funds."

FIVE

SWIPE ME LEFT

Ted was certain beyond a shadow of a doubt they hadn't found the barbarian, yet, to look at Samuelson and Basa at the table, it was hard put not to think they both were barbaric.

Not that Ted was mister manners when he ate, neither was Lincoln. They both had this uncanny ability not to wipe their mouths or hands, claiming they'd have to do it when they were done eating anyhow. Ted was especially messy; his mother wiped his mouth so much he never noticed. Until the day Lincoln said, "Mom stop that. He's twenty years old."

Once in a while she'd still reach over. Ted would shrug it off as her need to be overprotective.

Their two guests, however, defied the word 'manners'. Both of them tore the chicken apart with their fingers. They lifted the potatoes with their hands and slurped the applesauce, all while making 'yum-yum' noises that were almost as hysterical as they were annoying.

Ted and Lincoln just stared.

Ted could understand Basa's immense hunger, she had been living on the streets for a couple days, but Samuelson had been eating everything in sight since he dropped into the attic.

Their mother didn't even notice. She sat back, giggling, moving her fingers on her phone. "Funny," she spoke to herself out loud. "Oh my. Nope." She shook her head. "Oh, Teddy, Aunt Sally said to ask you to look for seasons six through nine of *Dynasty*. You picked up the seasons Patrick Duffy wasn't in."

"Mom," Lincoln said. "Tell Aunt Sally if she is waiting to see Patrick Duffy in *Dynasty*, she will wait forever, he wasn't on *Dynasty*, he was on *Dallas*."

"Was he?" she asked. "Oh, that's right." She giggled. "How funny is that. I'm not telling her. She'll feel bad." She returned to her phone. "You kids enjoying the meal?"

"Uh, Ma, are you looking at them?" Ted asked.

"Madam," Basa said. "Your generosity in nourishing me is exceeded by your talents in preparing such a tasty feast. Whilst I am not convinced just yet, I am certain in time I can make great warriors of your male offspring."

"Ah, aren't you sweet," she said, still looking at her phone.

"Know full well," said Basa. "I would immediately give my blessing should you chose to wed my friend Samuelson."

"Wait. What?" Ted asked. "No."

"Although, I this Patrick Duffy you speak of surely will be jealous," Basa said. "Or Paxton, would be similarly disappointed."

"She has a voluptuous sister," Samuelson added. "Perhaps the years she has on Paxton, will not be a bother."

"Voluptuous, you say?" Basa asked.

"Oh!" Bea perked up. "Wait until I tell her. How do you spell voluptuous?"

"Stop," Ted said. "First, Aunt Sally has a husband and has had one for like thirty years. Second, dude, stop flirting with my mom."

Lincoln looked at Ted. "Stop being overprotective. She can date if she wants."

"Not the freaking Sam Elliott Wizard!" Ted blasted.

"I like Sam Elliott," Bea said. "And he's flattering. You know I lack confidence since I have the menopause."

"Mom," Lincoln said. "*Have* the menopause? You don't have the menopause. Not like it's a disease."

"You don't think?" Bea clanked up from her phone. "And if Mr. Wizard keeps it up, who knows, maybe I won't need this dating app. Although, this one is funny."

"What app?" Ted asked.

"Primder," she replied. "It's like that one app you young people use but for those older than fifty. We do that swipe thing."

"Ugh! You're on an old person hook up site?" Ted freaked.

"Dating, Teddy, and not hook up," she explained. "It makes things faster because we don't want to waste time with the going back and forth. Although I don't know why this guy is on, he seems young. Nice looking. But … listen to this. Prince needs his warrior princess to battle demons and more." She laughed. "Look at the clothing. Oh, even that's too strange for me. Swipe left."

"No!" Ted lunged grabbing for her phone. "Let me see."

"Teddy, I don't want to date him."

"It can't be," Lincoln said.

Ted looked down at the image then handed it to Samuelson. "Is that him?"

Samuelson looked at the same time Basa leaned in.

"Astonishing," Basa placed each one of her fingers in her mouth, pulling the chicken residue from them.

Lincoln cringed. "Dude, stop that. You're a girl."

"Female or no female. I am a hungry warrior." She licked her final finger and looked at the picture. "Amazing painting."

"Yes," Samuelson said. "That is him."

"That's him?" Lincoln asked with shock. "That's a selfie. He's on a senior hook up site. How long has he been here?"

"We'll find out." Ted took back the phone and swiped right.

<><><><><>

The doorbell rang.

Bea hurried down the hallway to the door, but Samuelson stopped her.

"Remember, his charms will overwhelm," Samuelson said. "Do not look too deeply into his eyes for more than a few moments or you will fall under his enchantment spell and be crippled with infatuation for nearly six marks of a candle."

"In all seriousness," Ted said. "Why doesn't Basa have the enchantment spell?"

Basa answered. "I am not a prince."

"No kidding."

"I do not jest with you."

"Stop." Lincoln held up his hand. "How exactly long is this …. six marks of a candle?"

"It all depends," replied Basa. "Are we talking narrow candles or thickened one? Six marks on a thickened one is nearly a night's rest. Six marks on a narrow is one mark on a thick."

"So which one is it?" Lincoln asked. "Thick or thin? We need to know this in case she stares into his—"

"Hello!" Bea opened the door. "Are you my Prince?"

"I am Paxton, Prince of Aberly, at your service," he bowed and lifted his head, looking up. "Samuelson." He grinned as he spotted the Wizard behind her. "You are here!" he stepped inside and smiled at Bea. "You wonderfully wicked temptress, calling us both."

"Hey!" Ted snapped.

"My friend," Samuelson gripped Paxton's arms. "Good of you to be here. Basalous is here as well."

"Three?" Paxton looked at Bea. "And one a woman. The talents you must have."

"Dude!" Ted barked.

"Well," Bea bashfully waved out her hand.

"Mom!" Ted's voice cracked.

"This is a wonderful reunion," said Paxton. "Samuelson, your appearance is matching a notable of this time. Has anyone spoken to you about your resemblance to the icon Samuel Elliott?"

"Wait," Lincoln said. "If you know about Sam Elliott, how long have you been here?"

<><><><><>

"Nearly one full moon cycle," Paxton recounted his story around the dining table. "I knew by the lack of destruction I had arrived ahead of the others in the quest."

"More wine?" Bea asked.

"Please, thank you kind woman." Paxton pushed his glass forward. "Unfortunately, this world was not kind to me. I arrived on a river's edge, near many sea vessels. There were these carriages with flashing lights of red and blue."

"Office Bill Smith!" Basa shouted. "He arrives in those."

"There were many Office Bill Smiths," said Paxton. "After removing my weapon and shield, they took me and many others to a room where we sat. They told me I was being apprehended for smuggling a mind-altering substance. I was offended. I smuggle no such thing. I feigned loss of memory brought on by an attack of beggars and gypsies. They released me from the dungeon and sent me to an institution, where the continuous loss of memory provided me with a warm bed, three meals and gatherings where we made wonderful drawings and crafts."

"Quick thinking my friend," Samuelson said.

"So, after the drug bust you faked amnesia? Ted asked. "Oh, that is the oldest trick in the book and everyone falls for it, because there is no way to prove amnesia. I remember once, I was watching old episodes of *Days of Our* lives from nineteen eighty-six and Sami fakes her amnesia."

"Ted," Lincoln said his name sharply. "Please stop with the soap operas. Thank you," he faced the Prince. "It still doesn't explain how you ended up on Primder."

"Yes, I met a friend in the institution. His name was Lawrence, he was a kind soul to me. He brought me into his home. I knew if my friends were not here, they would be shortly, and I asked him how to connect with people rather quickly. He helped me secure the telecommunication device."

"What wit!" said Basa. "You are very cunning, it is no wonder you are enchanting."

"Thank you. Apparently, this world calls it 'hooking up'. I had no luck finding you until today. However, the women of this world are very friendly. Each investigation, the woman offered her body to me."

The Wizard laughed like a teenager, in almost a cheering way.

Basa gave a scolding look. "I fail to see how this is cause for triumph. If Paxton would say they have joined the battle, then I would cheer."

51

Samuelson glanced at her. "It is something you shall not understand."

"Nor do I wish to."

"So this Primder," Samuelson said. "Has been kind to you."

"I do have a face … book profile, as well."

Bea reached out and placed her hand on his. "I will have to befriend you on that. I have one too."

"Lovely lady," he looked at her. "I would be honored." After a moment, he finished his wine and stood. "All light pleasantries aside, Samuelson, I can not locate the Barbarian or Fairy. Surely, they are in this world by now. You must conjure your abilities and try to find them. We have been given a reprieve as of now. But the fiery rage of the draconem is at hand, the Maniacal Master will begin his reign here. And while this world is far more advanced than ours, they are ill equipped mentally to handle what awaits them."

"I will begin tonight," Samuelson said. "Even if it drains me for a while."

"Good."

"Shall we retreat," Basa said. "To the outdoors and speak around a fire of our plans?"

"A fine idea," Samuelson said. "Teddy and Lincoln shall join us."

Paxton faced Bea. "My lady, we bid you a fare good night, I hope we have not burdened you with our presence."

"You can burden me all you want," she said slowly, staring at him.

"Mom?" Ted called her attention.

Samuelson slipped close to Ted and whispered. "Perhaps you should take your mother somewhere safe for a bit," he said. "Sadly, she has been enchanted."

Lincoln shook his head. "I'm calling Aunt Sally to watch her," he said. "This keeps getting weirder by the second." He pulled out his phone, continuously shaking his head at his mother who stared enamored at the Prince.

SIX

AT FIRST PASS

It baffled him. Lincoln wondered if he was missing something. He got a message from his Aunt Sally that Mr. Wizard had news, yet when Lincoln arrived at his mother's house after his shift, Samuelson wasn't in the room. But Ted sat between Paxton and Basa, explaining to the other world visitors the fundamentals of soap operas.

"If my life was a visual tale," said Paxton. "It would be a soap opera, but it would pause for informative moments."

"Yes," Ted replied.

"How convenient," Paxton said in awe. "You have a problem, you just pause it. Wonderful concept, I wish we could pause the battle ahead of us."

"What I do not get," Basa said, "is how the small people are in there. Do they live there, is this their lives?"

"Slayer, you foolish woman!" Paxton snapped. "It's a mystical box that projects images."

In the doorway between the living room and dining room, Lincoln stood with Sally. "And they've been like this all day?" he asked her

"All day. He has gone through a different soap opera every hour."

"That's insane."

"These are your new friends, now …" Sally folded her arms. "Your mother may live in oblivion, but let me get this straight. Your new friends consist of a Prince, a Slayer and a Wizard who looks like Sam Elliott."

"You can't blame the Sam Elliott thing on us," Lincoln replied. "But yes, in a nutshell that's it."

"And you had room to make fun of me confusing *Dynasty* and *Dallas*. I'll have you know," Sally said. "Lots of people confuse them."

A few thumping footsteps, and Samuelson raced into the room. "Ah, Lincoln you are here. I am …" He paused to lean into him and sniffed. "You have a strange substance smell to you."

"It's called fries. What's up?" Lincoln asked.

"I have been reaching to the universe and I believe it has given me a clue to the whereabouts of the Barbarian and Fairy."

Sally blinked several times quickly. "And we're adding a Barbarian and Fairy now."

"Why, yes," Samuelson said. "They are not as charming as us."

"I wouldn't think so," Sally said. "Anyhow, I have to get back to my color, she's done under the dryer now. Good luck."

"Thank you," Samuelson told her then faced Lincoln when she left. "This house is blessed with wonderful women."

"Sam, what was the clue?"

"Do the words peeping Toms on the mount mean anything to you?"

"Um … yeah," Lincoln said puzzled. "It's a … a special club men go to in Mount Washington."

"A mountain club for men?"

"Well, Mount Washington is on this side of the river and has a great view of the city. Peeping Toms is a club there. Why?"

"That was my message. That is where we can find the Barbarian and the Fairy."

"Why does that not surprise me." Lincoln walked over to the coffee table, lifted the remote and shut off the television.

All three on the couch vocally protested.

"Link!" Ted held out his hand. "Why did you do that?"

"We have to go. Sam thinks he knows where the Barbarian and Fairy are."

"For real?" Ted stood up. "Where?"

"Peeping Tom's in Mount Washington."

"Sweet."

The Prince stood as well. "We've located the remainder of the band of heroes?"

"We must go!" Basa rose from the couch. "At once. *Days of our Lives* can wait until we return."

Samuelson stopped her. "I am afraid Basalous, you can not go. It is called Peeping Toms. Lincoln has informed me this is a mountain club for men."

"And we," Paxton said. "Are men. You are not."

"And it is comments like that show you truly are a man of simple wit and minimal skill," she snapped. "Am I not fit to be around men? Young Ted." She faced him. "You are wise. Does your world truly feel that a woman such as myself am not good enough to be at Peeping Toms?"

"Oh, no." Ted shook his head. "You can go. In fact, they'd love you there."

"Thank you, my new friend Ted," she said. "I will make you proud and show you how much I belong at Peeping Toms."

Ted smiled. "Sweet. I can't wait to see."

Lincoln backhanded him. "We'll take my car," Lincoln said. "Shit. Wait. Won't work. If they're there, we'll never fit."

"If they're there. We'll split up. We'll take an Uber back," Ted suggested.

"An Uber?" Lincoln asked. "You want to put half this bunch in an Uber?"

Ted shrugged.

"I'll borrow Aunt Sally's minivan." Lincoln waved for the group to follow.

"I'll catch up," Ted told him. "Go on, I'll be right back."

"Where are you doing?" Lincoln asked.

"Up to my room." Ted backed up. "If we're going to Peeping Toms, I'm grabbing the KFC bucket. There's eighty-two dollars in ones."

Paxton asked, "What is this Peeping Toms?"

"It's a special sort of club, you'll see. But it makes no sense," Lincoln said. "Why in the world would they be there?"

<><><><>

Outside the club, the sun was bright, but inside it was hard to tell it was even daytime.

The music played loudly; the atmosphere was dark.

"It feels as if we stepped into yet another world," said Samuelson.

"Yep. Wait," Lincoln said.

A woman dressed in a short-cropped tee shirt that fell barely below her breasts and extremely short shorts approached them. "All together or paying separately?"

"Madam," Samuelson said. "It appears most of your clothing is missing."

"You'll have that." She smiled.

"I guess together," Lincoln replied.

"Five of you, that will be One twenty-five."

"Oh my God, one twenty-five." Lincoln pulled out his wallet and handed her the credit card. "You guys better hope the world is ending. A hundred bucks to get in here." He signed on the key-pad and replaced his card.

"Drink coupons," she handed him cards. "Have fun."

"Thanks." Lincoln led the way into the club where it was even darker. It wasn't just one stage, several stages, like fashion run-ways, extended into the table areas.

Several women danced on those stages, they wore only skimpy bottoms and no tops.

"Aw, man," Ted said. "It's before eight. No full nudity."

Samuelson tapped Lincoln on the shoulder. "Why are these women swinging on a beam with no clothing."

Basa answered. "Is it not obvious? They are training their bod-ies to be nimble in battle, they use the beam to practice how they will swing and launch their bodies to the enemy. And they are brave, they do so while vulnerable, without the shielding of cloth-ing. It makes me proud."

"Me, too," said Ted. "Plus, men like it."

"I like it," Paxton said. "I shall get a closer look."

"No." Lincoln stopped him. "We all go in together. There aren't many here. Your friends shouldn't be hard to find. I don't understand how they have the money for this."

"Oh, the Fairy can produce coin," Samuelson said. "Once we visited a pub and it was unending."

"Swell. What are their names?" Lincoln asked.

"The Fairy is Ignatius."

"Ignatius as in a man?" Lincoln asked.

59

"Yes, a rare occurrence, but he is male. And the Barbarian is Bruce."

"Bruce? Bruce?" Lincoln asked in shock. "All of you have these strange names and his is Bruce? Okay, let's go find them." He noticed that the others were all staring in awe of the dancers. "Guys, come on, let's go and get out of here."

"There!" Samuelson pointed. "There they are. Bruce, he sits by the dancing woman wearing the star over her field of pleasantries. The Fairy is at another table nearby."

The Slayer, the Prince and of course, Ted – holding firmly to the bucket – rushed inside.

Without a doubt, it was the Barbarian, how did Lincoln miss him? No one sat around him. He was alone at the table, with several pitchers of beer, and was getting plenty of attention from the dancers. Even sitting down, he looked huge. The fur vest he wore didn't help. His arms were large and muscular, and his trapezoids looked like they came to his ears. Though it was dark, Lincoln could clearly see his bald head was covered in tattoos.

Lincoln and Samuelson caught up to the others.

"Bruce," Samuelson called his name.

Bruce turned. "Friends" He shouted, then charged out a cry of joy that sounded like a roar. He jumped to his feet and embraced Samuelson, Paxton and Basa. "Have we new people?" he asked.

"We do," Samuelson replied. "They are here to help with the quest. And we must go Bruce. We must prepare."

"We must drink first!" he lifted a pitcher, chugged nearly the entire thing then slammed it to the table. "Yes! Ladies, greet my friends."

Lincoln winced. He watched his brother as a dancer approached. Ted was completely engrossed. It reminded Lincoln of when they'd go to the movies: Ted would stare forward, never blinking and blindly reaching into the popcorn bucket. Instead of popcorn, now Ted pulled out ones and like a zombie, just handed the bills to the dancers.

"Where's the Fairy?" Lincoln asked.

"What?" Samuelson replied.

"The Fairy!" Lincoln shouted over the music and barbarian cheers. "You said he was here. Where?"

"He's right here!"

"Where? I don't see him."

Suddenly, Lincoln felt a sharp pain to his shin. Upon realizing he had been kicked, he looked around. Did someone just dart, kick him and run?

"I'm right here you moron," said the male voice.

Lincoln lowered his gaze. He stood before him, wearing a trench coat that was far too big for his short stature body. The dark wavy hair and goatee looked intimidating. "Are you the Fairy?" Lincoln asked.

"Are you the asshole?"

Samuelson cleared his throat nervously. "Ignatius can be quite curt."

"I'll say." Lincoln shook his head. "I'm sorry. I'm Lincoln."

"And I'm annoyed. We have been here for twenty-four hours. Straight. Do you know a barbarian can consume sixty-three pitchers of beer and still not be intoxicated?" Ignatius said. "And you Samuelson, apparently you've been in town long enough to get a style change."

"I'm confused," Lincoln said. "He really doesn't talk like the rest of you."

"A Fairy can adapt to any environment seamlessly and quickly," Samuelson replied.

"And I'm tired of being here. Can we go now?" Ignatius asked, "Because I don't think either of you know what it's like to sit here for an entire day straight wearing a trench coat so I don't call attention to my wings and tail!"

"Tail?" Lincoln asked. "You have a tail."

"Oh, you're so close, pal, to me just laying you out."

"What did I do?" Lincoln asked. "I didn't know fairies had tails."

Samuelson held up his hand to Ignatius. "He knows not much of us, it is our job to teach him. We need him and his brother to help rid this world of the Maniacal Master and get us home."

"Oh, oh, so he's the bastard that opened the portal."

"Something like that. Lincoln, you shall get the others and we will wait just by the scantily dressed tax collector woman out there." Samuelson pointed.

"Oh, you want me to get them?" Lincoln exhaled. "Fine. Easier said than done." He made his way to the Barbarian's table.

They were hooting and hollering, throwing money at the dancers.

Except for Slayer; she stood to the side, arms folded and chest out like a proud mama. She cheered them on as well, but in her own way. "You are working very hard. You will represent our species well in the battle. Swing. That is correct. Swing. Swing."

"Okay, okay, okay, Slayer ..." Lincoln pulled her back. "That's not how we ... or what you say. Never mind. Gentlemen," Lincoln called out. "It's time to go home now."

Bruce the Barbarian turned and glared at Lincoln.

"Okay." Lincoln inched back. "Maybe not."

After fifteen minutes of Lincoln failing to make headway, Ignatius charged into the lounge, grabbed Bruce by the ear and shouted with authority. "Get your ass off that chair it's time to go home you big dumb maniac."

And instantly, Bruce gave in, meekly following the Fairy from the club.

He stepped outside and grunted and groaned when his eyes didn't adjust to the light very quickly.

"We're right here," Lincoln pointed to the blue van with patched up rust spots.

Ignatius looked at it. "This is our carriage? What the hell is this thing?"

"It's called a minivan and it's all we have that can hold us all right now," Lincoln replied. He unlocked the van with a press of the automatic locks and slid open the side door. "Everyone in."

Stepping back, Lincoln noticed Ted.

His brother clutched the bucket, staring down to it.

"What's wrong with you?" Lincoln asked.

"There were two hundred and four dollars in here, in various bills," Ted answered.

"What's left?"

Ted showed him the empty bucket.

"You spent it all? What the hell were you thinking?"

"I don't know. I was like hypnotized, I just kept giving it away."

"Serves you right." Lincoln took the empty bucket and hit Ted on the head with it. "Next time..."

A large crack of thunder caused a complete halt to everyone and the sky instantly turned gray.

"Ah," said Bruce. "That's better. I can see."

"That was really fast," Ted said. "There wasn't a cloud in the sky."

Lincoln saw Ignatius move slowly down the sidewalk to the back end of the van. As soon as he did that, a shadow fell over them and it wasn't a cloud.

A flapping sound preceded the loud screeching roar and even though they were high in the sky, both Lincoln and Ted ducked as three dragons soared overhead.

Their location on that sidewalk in Mount Washington afforded them a view that tourists would gather to see.

A perfect view of the entire city.

A perfect view of the dragons as they flew together, all three. They parted ways just as they reached the city, dividing in synchronization. Their wings steady and each lifted their heads in another roar, before widening their mouths and releasing a rage of fire to the buildings below.

Lincoln stumbled back, immediately grabbing for his brother to make sure he was close.

On that hillside where they stood, people panicked. Cars honked horns, tires screeched as brakes slammed and vehicles collided into each other.

It was instant pandemonium but nothing compared to what lay below at the foot of the city.

The dragons didn't just spray fire, they blasted it as a weapon. Concrete buildings exploded from the force of the hits, one after another. Everything became engulfed in flames so easily. Burning with such an intensity that the city was quickly created a veil of black smoke.

The attack and destruction was swift and the three dragons rose from the smoke and flames and flew off disappearing into the cloud covered sky just as swiftly as they had appeared.

The brothers stood stunned.

It didn't matter what they had been told about the opening of the portal, the war that dropped from the sky upon them. Being told about it didn't have the impact of seeing it.

It wasn't just a tale. It was real.

The apocalypse had begun.

SEVEN

HOME BASE

"Jesus, mom, come on." Ted held the phone to his ear. "Answer. Please."

Lincoln grew impatient with the number of vehicles suddenly on the road, everyone trying to run to go somewhere.

"Did you try Aunt Sally?" Lincoln asked.

"No, but Paxton is." Ted looked to the back seat.

Paxton held up his phone. "I am continuously attempting the voluptuous one's communication device."

"Samuelson," Lincoln said. "How in the word do you beat these things in the middle of the city?"

"You do not," Samuelson answered. "You must wait until they rest and find reprieve. Attack them in repose, but as I said, he will create more. We must find him."

"And some," added the Fairy.

"Wh-what does that mean." Lincoln asked nervously. "And some."

"The bastard's crafty," replied Ignatius.

"Great beasts to fight," said Bruce. "Yes!"

"Is that what you guys were doing when you fell through?" Lincoln asked.

Ted grunted. "Pick up the phone, Mom!" He attempted to call again.

"Keep trying," Lincoln told him.

"To answer your question," Samuelson said. "We were in fact on a very positive trail to the Maniacal Master's lair, having just finished a questline in a village. A great storm began and the sky swirled. The draconem appeared and were brought in first, then each of my band of heroes, one-by-one, shot upward to the sky."

"Except me," Ignatius said. "I grabbed Bruce away from that tree. We were going up anyhow, we didn't need the tree with us."

"I knew exactly what was happening," said Samuelson. "I knew it was a portal. I heard the Maniacal Master's evil laugh. It echoed and disappeared just as I, the last one, was brought in. As soon as I crossed I was in your cottage."

"Excuse me, Warrior Lincoln," Basa leaned forward and tapped him on the shoulder. "Why are we not moving?"

"Because all these people decided to run," Lincoln said. "Where they are headed, I don't know. Now we're stuck in traffic."

"Perhaps they are rushing to join the quest," Basa said.

"Somehow I doubt that," replied Lincoln.

"Did this transport not tell all to stay inside?" Basa asked.

"What?" Lincoln was confused.

"This transport, it speaks in male tongue. It said to stay inside. I heard it speak."

"Yes!" Bruce blasted. "We should go protect the scantily dressed women. Candy needs my protection."

"No," Lincoln said. "She doesn't need your protection. Just sit."

"Link, I'm worried about Mom," Ted said. "They aren't answering. I know we watched those things disappear but we don't know where they went. We could walk home faster."

"I know. I know, but what can we do?" Lincoln said. "We can't just up and fly."

There was weird wave of silence, that seemed to flow from the back of the van. Both Lincoln and Ted turned around and looked.

Everyone was staring at the Fairy.

"Fine. Fine. Alright," Ignatius folded his arms in frustration. "I'll shape shift us."

"Wait," Lincoln said. "We've been in traffic for a half hour, desperately trying to reach our mother and you had the ability the whole time to get us home."

"I also have the ability to permanently turn you into a frog," Ignatius said. "You don't see me jumping on that ... Yet."

Ignatius snapped his finger.

<><><><>

The minivan gently lowered to the street directly in front of the house.

69

Ted wasted no time getting out and looking at the house. "It's fine. They may be in the basement." He turned to wait for Lincoln and saw the minivan.

He knew it was a bumpy ride, but Ted was so concerned for his mother and Aunt he really didn't pay attention to what the others were screaming about.

The side of the minivan was scorched, windows were broken, and large holes graced the driver's side.

Lincoln slammed the driver's door and it dropped to the ground. If that wasn't bad enough, the moment Samuelson slid open the side door, it kept going, right off the track where it teetered for a second them fell over.

"What …" Lincoln faced Ignatius. "What part of making us look like a dragon was a good idea?"

"Hey! How was I supposed to know your helicopters would shoot at us? I got us here safe and …" He looked at the house. "Is this where we are staying? It's very …"

"Don't!" Lincoln cut him off. "Nothing negative about my mom's house."

"I was going to say closed in, that's all."

Tired of waiting, Ted walked hurriedly to the house. He called out as soon as he entered. "Mom!"

He heard voices, in fact they were loud coming from the shop. Two female voices, were they his mother and aunt? It didn't sound like them.

"I needed to tell you. He was burned in the accident. His face," said the one woman.

"Oh my God. His face?"

"All I know is he's had surgery ..."

Ted bolted into the shop, obviously they were talking about someone he knew burned in the dragon attack. The second he stepped in the shop, he saw that wasn't the case. His mother and Sally and two other women were watching the television, it played loudly, showing a scene from *Dynasty*.

"Teddy?" his mother looked at him in shock. "You look upset. What's wrong? We were just watching ..."

"*Dynasty*, yeah, Season three Episode nineteen. Mom ... aren't you watching the news?"

"No." She shook her head.

"Honestly," Sally said. "We have been all engrossed for hours. So much so we forgot about the perm on Mrs. Lane."

Mrs. Lane looked up. "I don't mind super short hair now."

"Ma." Ted lifted the remote, shut off the VHS and changed the mode to television.

Immediately, the image was of a burning Pittsburgh.

"Holy shit." Sally jumped up. "That's our city."

"Yeah, yeah it is."

Lincoln rushed into the shop. "Everyone okay?"

His mother, aunt and two other women just watched the television in shock.

"When did this happen?" his mother asked.

"Not long ago," Ted replied. "We were up on Mount Washington. We saw the whole thing. We were there."

Sally asked. "Was it a terror attack?"

"No." Ted shook his head. "Dragons."

<><><><>

Bea had taken a break, she had to, she couldn't watch the news anymore. It wasn't just Pittsburgh. In the span of two hours. Erie, Cleveland then Columbus were hit. All three cities burned out of control and last reported the beasts were moving toward Charleston, despite the air force having announced that they had killed three of the monsters.

She returned to the kitchen to start gathering food items. Was she really leaving a house she lived in for twenty-five years?

Sally had borrowed her car to go home. She wouldn't be long, she couldn't be. Lincoln told her they had to evacuate.

And go where?

She started at the can of SpaghettiOs with Franks wondering when she bought them. Was it the most recent trip or was it right after Teddy moved back in?

"Mom?" Ted called her. "Are you okay in there?"

Bea set down the can and walked back to the living room. She sighed in relief when the television was off. "Yes, thank you." She looked at the newcomers in her house. Sam, Basa, Paxton, Bruce and Iggy. "Where is Teddy?"

"He's upstairs," Lincoln replied. "He's been up there a while. He said there was something he had to do."

Bea nodded. "So what now?"

Ignatius walked to her. "We will get you to a safe place. You and your sister and her husband."

"What about my sons?"

"They will be helping us," said Ignatius

"We will make them warriors!" Bruce chanted.

"No!" Bea said. "No you won't, my boys are not fighters."

"Well, your boys started this," said Ignatius. "And they're the only ones that can finish it."

"My dear Primder connection," Paxton stepped to her. "Have no fear, we will protect them and train them. I can enchant any beast."

"And I ..." Basa raised a sword. "Can slay them, with Bruce as my comrade. We all have abilities that are the maximum achieved in our world."

Samuel looked at her and held her eyes, "collectively, we are one mighty force."

"But my boys," Bea said, "how is this their doing?"

"Technically," Lincoln answered, "you started it Mom. You decided to one up us, win us the flaming sword, which helped complete the quest that opened the portal."

"Wait, that was all true?" Bea asked.

"Mom, we told you this when we introduced you to the Wizard. I knew you reacted too calmly."

"Of course, I did," Bea said. "I thought you boys were teasing me and making up a story so he could stay. I have that open door policy here."

"Mom, you were way too calm. It didn't even hit you as strange that he just showed up and that I said he was a wizard?"

"No." Bea shook her head. "I thought he was related to Joan and George Wizard of McKeesport. I had no idea he was a real wizard. Joan and George are a strange bunch, you know, they just show up for barbecues unannounced."

"Oh my God," Lincoln groaned. "Just finish getting ready. Pack something."

"And no worries my fine woman specimen," Samuelson said. "You will never once be in danger."

"Thank you," Bea said. "Should I bring my scissors and clippers in case somebody needs a haircut?"

"Mom!"

"What Lincoln! Don't yell at me. I am still processing this and ... people need to feel good about themselves even in the face of the apocalypse."

"I doubt that."

"Yeah, well, tell me about it when your bangs get too long, hang in your eyes and you can't see to fight the dragons." Bea spun in a huff and left the room.

Ted zippered the backpack. It was one that he hadn't seen since the fifth grade. He knew it had to be in his closet. He had never thrown it out and his mother had never changed the room. He was glad he had found what he was looking for. Perhaps the others would think it was dumb, but to Ted, it was at least something he could do since he wasn't a mighty slayer.

He shouldered the bag and carried it down the stairs.

Everyone looked as if they were ready to go.

"I thought we weren't leaving until nightfall," Ted said.

"We're not. Where were you?" Lincoln asked.

"So, I started thinking, right? What if the new game wasn't supposed to be there at the end of our *Wind and War* quest? I think it's someone else's game; the Master from your world, perhaps. Maybe he wanted to piggyback on the popularity of *Wind and War*, hacked it somehow, and lured us in."

"This is a possibility," said Ignatius. "Every time we complete a quest line in our world, he adds a new, tougher, one."

Ted snapped his finger. "Exactly. He keeps you hooked on his game. Next level. You beat that one."

"Dude," Lincoln said. "For all we know, it can be some kid in Iowa who released a video game that is actually controlling reality."

"Brat." Ted muttered.

"Me or the kid?" Lincoln pulled a face as if offended, then pointed. "What's in the bag?"

"The books Aunt Sally got me. When I was ten, she thought I was into all those fantasy video games and she bought me the books that taught me about the games and how to beat the levels.

She figured if I was playing games, I should read." He waved out his hand pointing at the others. "Wizard, Slayer, Barbarian, Prince and Fairy. Sounds like a fantasy book to me. I grabbed them all. Maybe there is something in there that can help us figure out the next move."

"That is an awesome idea."

Paxton stepped forward. "I know not what you speak. Perhaps you can enlighten me after we travel to the obliterated village."

"I'm sorry what?" Ted asked.

"It is our duty," Paxton said. "To assist with those who may need help after an attack, to free them from danger."

Basa added. "Who knows what vile creature will rise from the ashes."

"Let's go get the creatures. I can smell them out!" Bruce said.

"Smell them?" Lincoln asked.

"Yes, and I am super strong."

"I … I believe that," Lincoln said.

"What about our mom?" Ted asked.

"I will stay here," Samuelson said. "To help her gather the supplies and move her out at nightfall with the voluptuous one and her husband."

"Don't worry." Ignatius said. "I'll know where they are and will go. I will manifest what they need. Samuelson will get them on their way and we will join them after we check the village for those who need help."

"Um …" Ted scratched his head. "You know how big the Village of Pittsburgh is, right?"

Ignatius nodded. "It doesn't matter. Our time to help is limited, we too will have to get people out before dawn."

"What happens at dawn?" Ted asked.

"They come back for round two," Ignatius said. "They always come back."

EIGHT

BURNING VILLAGE

In a city of hundreds of bridges, only one bridge remained unscathed.

How that happened, Ted didn't know. The abilities of the Portal Five, as Ted named them in the car, were amazing. Individually they were cool, but together they were like the fantasy version of the Avengers. Only, at the present time he didn't know if any of them could fly.

With a wave of his hand over the air before they left, Samuelson was able to share his 'know-all' ability by showing them an aerial view of the city and the destruction brought upon it.

Even though from a distance and from what the news showed it appeared the entire city was aflame, it wasn't. Most of it was, but the burning and fire seemed contained to three large strips. Each dragon delivering its own torch of death. The crumbling buildings smothered a lot of the flames, causing a smoldering that released a steady flow of smoke into the air.

"This shit you saw," said Ignatius on their drive there. "It won't be like that for long. Once the smoke settles and the sky starts to get light again, they won't do a fly by like today, they'll blast it."

"Sadly," Paxton added. "We have seen this before."

"Many times," Basa said. "Since the arrival of the draconem and the beast creature that guards the forest, we have to lead those who remain out of the flames."

"They suffer," Bruce said.

Lincoln asked. "And do what with them?"

"We have healers," Paxton said. "Even if they do not survive, their death is better in peaceful surroundings than burning to ashes, would you not agree? You do not have healers?"

"Oh, we have them," Lincoln said. "I just don't know how we're supposed to get them to the hospitals as we call them."

"Leave that to me.," Ignatius said. "If we can think it, I can manifest it."

Ted and Lincoln lived six miles south of the city, through the tunnel that was set at the end of the only remaining bridge.

A steady flow of people walked from tunnels that were jam packed on both sides with cars going outbound.

They left the car parked on side street and walked against the traffic into the city.

Ted expected to get weird glances: people looking at them strangely because they walked toward the destruction instead of away from it. But the faces he saw were those of people confused, in pain. They had injuries; skin blackened with soot. They held on to each other for support. Some cried, some were silent.

The cars and trucks were all abandoned on the bridge, people had just left them behind.

Midway on the bridge, Ignatius hurried to the railing, he climbed up to get a better look.

"Whoa. Whoa!" Lincoln hurried to him. "Be careful you can fall."

"Really?" Ignatius said. "You do know I'm a Fairy. I have wings."

"What are you doing?"

"Looking at the river. All those boats."

"It's people trying to get away. They can't drive," Lincoln said.

"And go where?" Ignatius shook his head and climbed down. "I hope they get somewhere soon because when the draconem come back, they're sitting ducks. No pun intended to the water."

"That was bad."

Ignatius shrugged.

Ted didn't say much. He was at a loss for words and mainly because his mind was filtering and processing all that was going on. He was certain his brother was doing the same thing. It didn't make sense. Lincoln said earlier that there had to be a logical explanation. Ted was bound and determined to figure that out, even if it didn't make sense.

At the end of the bridge they saw a lone police officer, waving people in a direction to evacuate. There was the steady sound of fighter jets flying overhead from the airfield. Flashing lights of ambulances were seen in the distance, moving people to one of the hospitals that remained on the city side of the river.

If the Portal Five were correct, none of the transporting would matter. The dragons would return to finish everything off. That was unless the Air Force got them, which was possible.

"Officer Bill Smith!" Basa called out, excitedly. "Officer Bill Smith!"

The officer turned around, the look on his face showed how shocked he was to see Basa.

"You have survived the carnage that besieged the village," Basa said.

"I ... I did."

"Then you are wise and strong. You must join our quest. Tonight, we begin our journey to find the nest. We may not be able to stop a second coming of them to this village, but we save another village. Join us. Bruce will wrangle them and I will slash their bellies releasing the souls of those they consumed."

"They consumed?" the officer asked.

Ignatius nudged Basa and spoke through clenched jaws. "They haven't consumed anyone yet. That's later, you know."

Basa cringed. "I misspoke. My apologies."

"What are you doing here?" the officer asked.

Lincoln spoke up, "We want to help with rescue attempts."

"Normally I would tell you to turn back," the officer looked at Basa, then Paxton and Bruce. "But I have this odd feeling you guys might actually help. They can use some hands moving rubble from the courthouse. It collapsed and people are trapped."

"Tell me kind sir," Bruce said. "How big would the stones of rubble be? Twenty, thirty feet round."

"Not that big, more like ..." the Officer widened his hands a couple feet apart. "That big I would assume. It's rubble."

"Then that is no problem. I can handle it," Bruce said. "Onward. We must save the smashed villagers. Where is this court ... house?"

Officer Bill slowly point back.

"I know where it is," Ted stepped ahead.

"Of course you do," Lincoln said.

"What is that supposed to mean?"

"Dude, I'm not the one that took a six months sabbatical from life and discovered juvenile delinquency at thirty years old."

Both Ted and Lincoln stopped walking when they heard a loud gasp come from Basa.

"What now?" Ted asked.

"You are thirty years old?" Basa asked.

"Yeah." Ted started walking again.

"I'm thirty-two," Lincoln said.

"And you are only mere mortals?" asked Basa. "Not secret Wizards?"

"No, why?" asked Ted.

"You must have led such an easy life to be so old and look so youthful. Even I have had life's battles grace my face with lines of age," Basa said. "It is no wonder your mother worries so much for your safety. When we see her this evening, I will assure her we will be careful with two in such advanced years."

Lincoln shook his head and caught up to Ted. "In all the soaps you watched, have ever seen characters as weird as this?"

"Nope," Ted replied. "If I did. I'd stop watching."

<><><><><>

It was pointless, Ted thought. They walked the two blocks to the courthouse. The smoke still lingered in the air, there was an orange tone to everything and it was hot, extremely hot.

There were a dozen workers: some construction, a couple firemen and a police officer.

"Stay back," the fireman told them. "Just stay back. It's dangerous."

Bruce, arms folded just shook his head. "Look at them as they move one stone at a time."

"You got a better idea, Pal?" the fireman snapped.

"Yes. That large stone there." Bruce pointed. "Would it not be wiser if we moved that out of the way?"

"Oh, sure, sure," the fireman answered sarcastically. "It's would be a big help. Unfortunately, we don't have the equipment," his voice began to raise. "And no one can move a couple ton piece of concrete!"

"That is a dilemma for you. No wonder it still sits there," Bruce said. "Come Basalous and my Prince, guide me as I move the stone."

He moved forth.

"Are you nuts?" the fireman shouted. "We have people trapped. We can't have you pissing …" His hand was outward and he just froze.

Bruce positioned himself one the edge of the wall, slipping his hand behind it. Within seconds he lifted it upright.

Lincoln's eyes widened. "Is he … is moving that?"

Ignatius nodded. "He is strong."

"That's beyond strong."

"He conquers mythical creatures," Ignatius said. "He's gotta have some strength for that."

Paxton and Basa served as a guide. Bruce had no problem moving the wall, but seeing where he was going was a different story. He walked with it back to the fireman.

"Where do I put this?" Bruce asked.

"Over … over there." The fireman said stunned.

"I will do that. What shall I move next?"

"Um, more big pieces?"

"Yes. I can do that." Then Bruce spoke in his loud chanting manner. "I will move more large stones!"

Lincoln winced.

Ted heard Ignatius snicker. "Not that rescue work isn't reward-ing. I get this whole hero thing, but it doesn't make sense that you do this."

"What do you mean?" Ignatius asked.

"Not that this is a waste of time. But why do you waste time doing this?" Ted asked. "Why aren't we right now actively headed toward their nest to be there before them."

"First, we don't know where the nest is. The Wizard has to help us with that. Once he does, then we go there."

"So why can't he help us now?" Ted asked. "I mean you are all powerful dragon hunters. Why can't he help now to find the Dragons before they strike again tomorrow?"

"I ... I don't know."

"Why does this matter?" Lincoln said.

"Because it doesn't make sense. We aren't needed here. We can try to save these lives by finding the dragons."

"Have you not paid attention to any of this?" Lincoln asked. "They slay the dragons, Maniacal Master only makes more."

"Three, then two, then three," said Ignatius.

Ted crinkled his brow. "Well, that doesn't make sense. He sends three, then two, then three dragons?"

"Ted!" Lincoln blasted. "What about any of this makes sense?"

"Hear me out." Ted raised his hand to Lincoln's eye level. "It all seems to be a pattern. If we can figure out the pattern ..."

"No, Ted, you're wrong."

"Not …." Ignatius eked out the word. "Necessarily. There is a pattern. Sort of. We battle, we win, the evil one creates more, they attack another place, we help, we battle, we win."

Ted nodded. "See?"

"See? See?" Lincoln snapped. "No, I don't see."

"They battle and win. The maniacal master makes more dragons. They battle, they win."

Ignatius interjected. "Don't forget the villages we help."

"That's my point. Why?" Ted asked. "Why stop when you're on a roll. Is it guilt because you couldn't save them?"

"Oh, way to rub it in," said Lincoln.

"No," Ignatius said. "How can we feel guilty about something we don't know is going to happen or where? Helping villagers makes us better. Stronger. We don't ask for rewards, but it seems we are given them. We need them because every battle gets tougher."

"Oh my God," Lincoln spoke in soft discovery. "Hidden weapons."

"Exactly," said Ted. "None of this is real. Okay, well, it is real in a real sense, but it isn't. All of this has a pattern because all of this is a game."

"Are you saying I'm not real?" Ignatius asked.

"Oh, you're real, you live and breathe but you exist on the other side of the portal," Ted explained. "There's a reason each battle gets tougher."

"It's another level," Lincoln said. "You said this before."

"I did and this is all helping it make sense." Ted nodded. "Ignatius, what exactly were you doing when you dropped through. I mean exactly."

"We just finished helping a village that was destroyed," Ignatius said.

"Oh, wow," Lincoln said. "Their power source"

Ted smiled. "Yep. And when we clicked enter on the game, we didn't inadvertently open a portal and sucked them in. It wasn't an accident," Ted said. "They … levelled up."

NINE

RETREAT

Eventually, after Bruce moved all the large objects, Ted and Lincoln joined the recovery efforts, standing in a human chain, handing over one rock to the next person, over and over.

They rescued nineteen people.

Aside from Bruce's keen ability to move heavy objects, something the fire fighters attributed to adrenaline, he also had an incredible sense of smell. Sniffing heavily, pointing out where they could find the injured.

Basa's ability would come in battle, something Ted looked forward to seeing. The Prince had the enchantment ability, and how that was going to come in handy with dragon battles remained to be seen.

To Ted, Ignatius had the coolest superpower: his ability to manifest new objects out of thin air. Money, food, vehicles. Everything but weapons, which made sense to Ted considering he was convinced they were playing some sort of game. There had to be limits on a power like that.

The Fairy conjured a vehicle that looked like a thin bus. It was super narrow and had one seat in each row. The mind play that went along with that was astonishing. Not a single person questioned the presence of a bus system that simply didn't exist. It carried over a hundred people, snaked through the rubble and headed north where Ignatius felt they'd be safe.

When the heroes finally left at nightfall, they had achieved a lot, but Ted was certain there were still loads of people left behind.

They returned to his mother's home to clean up. His Aunt Sally's broken-down minivan was gone. He figured the others must have fixed the doors. After grabbing a few more items, the six of them squeezed in Lincoln's SUV and they headed to where the Wizard, their mother, Aunt and Uncle were hunkered down in safety for the night.

Ignatius wasn't certain where they were going and Samuelson was horrible at leaving directions. His note simply said, 'follow the scent of safety, and there you will find us under the stars.'

Ted didn't know what that meant until Bruce called out directions: "Turn left, turn right. Don't turn."

Lincoln stated that he didn't think it mattered, the SUV seemed to be driving itself.

Which made sense to Ted, because nothing at that moment in time was in their control.

Samuelson stared at the bottle after just taking a drink, then with a smile he brought it to his lips and finished it. "This was the most refreshing ale I have ever had."

Sally's husband Bob sat in a folding lawn chair next to him. They, along with Sally and Bea, sat around a small campfire. "I made that myself," he said.

"How did you get the bubbles?" asked Samuelson.

"It's a secret." Bob winked. He rested his own beer on his belly. Not that Bob was heavy, he was just stout in the middle. He hadn't always been that way. He was a marine until he hit his thirties then started his own contracting company. The work started wearing him down. After turning over the physical aspect of his drywall business to his nephew, Bob didn't move that much. Between his wife's tailbone issues and his knees, there were days they needed to own stock in an ibuprofen company.

"Are you the owner of an inn?" Samuelson asked.

"No, but I build them."

"Bob the builder," Samuelson said. "Has a catchy ring to it."

"Lots of people say that."

"As a Wizard, I have had the chance to sample many ales. And this is by far the best."

"Thank you. Wizard huh?"

Samuelson nodded.

"Any relation to Joan and George Wizard out of Mckeesport."

"Not that I know of," said Samuelson.

Sally looked at Bea who stared at her phone. "Any word from the boys?"

Bea shook her head. "Nothing since we left. Phones went down."

"My dear lady," Samuelson said. "They are approaching now. So fear not and worry no more."

Bea and Sally looked.

Bob heard the sound of an approaching vehicle, and sure enough saw headlights.

"Okay." Lincoln clutched the steering wheel as he stopped. "We're in Mingo Park."

"Even better," Ignatius said. "We need to get some sleep. This is a good spot. Dawn comes early tomorrow."

"Ha!" Ted said. "Dawn comes early every day. And ... at the same time."

"No," Lincoln said. "It doesn't, it comes at different times."

"Dude, it does."

"No, Ted, it doesn't.

"Excuse me?" Paxton asked. "What exactly is a park?"

"It's a garden maintained and controlled by local governments: in this case, the state authorities run it."

"And they tax it?" asked Paxton.

"Taxes pay for it," Lincoln replied. "Yes. But I don't think we are allowed to camp here."

"Nature is for everyone." Basa opened the door. "I must greet the others before we rest for the night."

Ted asked his brother. "What's the problem?"

"First, it's a state park, they camped out in a camper. Where did they get that deluxe camper? They had a minivan."

Ignatius raised his hands. "I thought it was much better."

"It is," Ted said. "It's a really cool thing."

"I will change this to one as well."

"No!" Lincoln said. "I like my car, and they have a fire going. If the police come …"

"Link, I'm sure the police have other things on their mind."

"How is this safe?" Lincoln asked. "You said the dragons sleep in the woods."

"Mountainous areas," Ignatius said. "Even some with caves. Now can we go? I see there's a newcomer."

"Oh, dude, Uncle Bob. I love Uncle Bob." Ted opened the door. "I wonder if he's all caught up on *Secret Storm*. If they even showed it today." He stepped out.

Lincoln shook his head. "My brother has issues."

"Teddy!" Bob stood up and stepped from the circle of newcomers that surrounded him. "I am glad you're okay." He embraced him. "Meeting your new friends. Where's Link."

"Coming. Moping," Ted replied. "How's the knees?"

"Some days good, some days bad, but hey, I can't complain. I'm in pretty good shape for fifty-six years old."

When he said that, Basa exclaimed loudly in shock. "Fifty-six years old!" she stepped to Bob. "Did I hear you correctly? You say you are fifty-six years old?"

"I am."

"Then I apologize for not calling you by your rightfully earned title of Elderson." Basa gave a slight bow. "This world or time is kind. You look remarkable for a man of fifty-six."

"Why thank you," Bob said.

"I would take you for no more than thirty or thirty-three."

"Wow, I like this girl."

"I shall seek your wisdom often during my time on this foreign land. If you will excuse me Elderson, I must rest for battle."

"Against the dragons?" Bob asked.

"And some," replied Basa.

"I'd like to join that battle," Bob said. "In my youth I served my country and fought many battles."

"Your wisdom and experience would guide us much. Come Paxton. We have much to plan."

"Elderson," Paxton walked by him with a nod.

"Elderson," said Bruce as he walked by.

Samuelson stepped to Bob, following the others. "I too must turn in with my comrades. And my apologies, but I won't be referring to you as Elderson, Since I am much older."

"I ... can see that. Night Sam."

"Excuse them, they can be idiots," Ignatius told him.

"Aren't you different?" Bob replied.

"Is that dig to my height or my wings?" asked Ignatius.

"Neither," Bob replied. "The way you talk. You talk normal to me."

"Thanks, can I have one of those ales that I can smell?" Ignatius said. "Not in a barbarian way."

"Of course, help yourself. In the cooler." Bob lifted the lid, grabbed one for himself and handed one to Ignatius.

"Thanks. I'll take this to our camp." Ignatius lifted the beer and followed the others.

"Uncle Bob?" Ted asked. "You really want to join?"

"Actually, I do. Sit," Bob said.

Ted and Lincoln both sat by the fire on camp chairs that looked like they had been previously set up for them.

"I know you guys see me as fun Uncle Bob, the jolly uncle who watches television all the time," Bob said. "But I was a heck of a marine. Lots of missions."

"Uncle Bob," Ted said. "You weren't chasing dragons."

"But," Bea cut in. "He was chasing bad leaders. Diabolical men, like you're chasing now."

"Ma, please," Lincoln scoffed. "Totally different."

"Lincoln," Sally said. "My husband wants to go. Take him with you for goodness sakes. Your team is looking for warriors, my Bobby is a great warrior."

"And I look thirty." Bob winked.

94

"Okay." Ted raised his hands. "I would love to have you with us. It will be cool. But keep in mind, this bad guy is like no other. He's like, supernatural power evil."

"Why do you say that?" Bob asked.

"Um, we have dragons, and in case you didn't notice we have a Wizard."

"Yeah, well, I know and he's no relation to Joan and George."

"That's not what we're talking about," Ted said. "He created this … world that collided with us."

"I'm going to teach you two boys a new word. Ready? Manifestation."

"Uncle Bob?" Lincoln said. "We're like in our thirties. That 'new' word thing worked when we were nine, we're pretty much familiar with the word manifestation."

"I know that," Bob said. "This whole thing could be a manifestation. Because if you believe something so bad, want it so bad, you can manifest it. Look at me with my mole."

"I'm sorry what?" Lincoln asked. "Your mole."

Sally reached out and tapped Bob's knee. "Skin cancer."

"Skin cancer, right." Bob pointed at her. "For years and years, I kept telling your Aunt Sal that I was gonna get a mole that will be skin cancer."

"I told him, Bob, don't be ridiculous," Sally said.

"And I insisted it would show up," Bob said. "Sure as shit, I developed a brown spot and it ended up being skin cancer. I was twenty-eight years old."

"And you don't think serving as a marine in the desert had anything to do with that?" Lincoln asked.

"Nope. I manifested that."

Lincoln looked at Ted. "What do you think?"

"I think Uncle Bob got skin cancer from being in the desert sun. But ..." Ted replied. "He is right on the manifestation. I have been saying it all day. Whoever designed this game, and that's what we're in now, tapped into some sort of power and was able to manifest this all. We're in the live version of the game of their world."

"I love you brother, but I am not ruling out that this is some sort of alien thing. They came from the sky, dude, the sky. And the manifestation thing is a cop-out to find an explanation. Manifestations don't exist."

"And that's what we were told about Dragons, Fairies and Wizards yet ..." Ted shrugged. "Here we are. I'm going to figure this all out. You wait and see."

"Ah," Bea gushed. "That's my old Teddy."

"Thanks, Ma. And Link, keep in mind, there's never been a video game we couldn't beat," Ted said. "That's not gonna change now."

TEN

BOARD

It was a lot harder leaving his mom and Aunt Sally behind than Ted imagined. Neither one of them were physical fighters. Granted they were tough, strong and smart, but he worried.

Then, strangely enough, Officer Bill Smith showed up. A City of Pittsburgh police officer just randomly showed up eighteen miles south of the city. He brought the news that the authorities were able to evacuate the city and after that... something just made him drive south.

Ted would have truly believed his arrival was random and not influenced by Wizard had Mingo park, and the particular spot where they camped, it not been so far off the beaten trail.

Be that as it may, Ted was glad the policeman was there, even if it was temporary.

Officer Bill Smith truly wanted to join the warrior cause, but agreed to stay for the night as protection for Bea and Sally and said he would leave only to get his grandmother and bring her, as well, to this place of relative safety.

Despite how much Lincoln objected, Ignatius ignored his wishes and still transformed his brand new SUV into a long version of a van. Two bucket seats up front and bench seats in the back with a table for meetings on the road.

The Fairy promised to turn it back, but pointed out they needed something big enough to accommodate a crew which now included Uncle Bob.

"And we're sure our mom is safe?" Ted asked.

"I made sure of it," Samuelson said. "I brought Officer Bill Smith and placed a dome of protection over them."

"Do we know where we're going? And will we get there before dark?" Lincoln asked, looking into the rear-view mirror to speak to them as he drove. "Or is this van possessed and really driving on its own?"

Ignatius answered as he stood by the end of the table. "Both. So you don't need the map Uncle Bob."

"That's not why I'm marking it," Bob answered.

"Because," Ignatius said. "Samuelson's 'know all' is guiding us to where we will find the draconem resting tonight."

"And there," said Basa, "We can slay them."

"If we're going to fight dragons." Bob said. "Would be nice if we could get our hands on weapons."

"We have weapons," Ignatius said.

"Not …" Bob motioned his hand. "Swords and stuff. Me, Ted and Link aren't experienced with those. I'm talking guns. Rifles. They'd take down Dragons."

"Oh, we have those," Ignatius said.

In his shock of hearing that, Lincoln jerked the wheel. "We have guns?"

Ignatius grabbed the back of Lincoln's seat to gain his balance again. "Yes, we have lots of your type of weapons, guns and stuff in a bag. Right in the back."

"Where … where did we get guns?" Lincoln asked.

"Where do you think?" Ignatius retorted. "The Village of Pittsburgh. When we went in and helped the villagers, we were rewarded."

"By whom?" Lincoln asked.

"I don't know," Ignatius replied. "The townspeople. Some scared guy pointed to it. The bag was left for us like it always is."

"See?" Ted reached over and nudged Lincoln. "Quest rewards."

"You're making me nervous standing there," Lincoln said to Ignatius. "Can you sit please."

"We're meeting," Ignatius said. "We need to meet before we arrive at the destination. I'm fine."

"How many dragons are there?" Bob asked.

"There would only be two this time," Ignatius replied. "Three attacked the city."

"And the air force shot them down," Bob replied. "I heard about that."

"But two showed up at dawn and attacked," Ignatius said. "He always makes more."

"Next time," Bruce spoke up. "There will be three." He held up four fingers.

Ignatius reached over and put one of Bruce's fingers down. "That's correct. It's a pattern. Three then two then three."

"Not three, then two, then three, then two?" Bob asked.

Ignatius shook his head. "We'll slay the two, but he'll send three more. Then when they die, three more. Actually … if your air force hadn't killed the three, we would be searching for three. Confusing, but we're used to it."

"So you just go around killing dragons?" Bob asked.

"And looking for the Maniacal Master," Ignatius said.

"Not only is he powerful," Samuelson said. "He is cunning. He stays one pace ahead of us."

Ted mumbled. "That's because he's the game writer."

"I'm sorry." Ignatius tugged his own ear. "The game writer?"

"Yeah," Ted answered. "The character you call Maniacal Master. The reason he's one step ahead of you always is that he's creating the battles."

"What makes you think so?" Ignatius questioned.

"Because you've never fought him? Right? Not even all-knowing Samuelson. Just …" Ted said. "Humor me."

"Ha!" shouted Bruce. "I shall do the honors. What did the hunter say when he met the maiden at the brothel?"

"Bruce," Ted tried to interrupt. "That's not what I—"

100

"Is this the breast you can give?" Bruce finished his joke. "Get it?" he laughed heartedly like everyone else. "The breast you can give."

Everyone laughed but Ted.

"You don't understand my friend?" Bruce asked. "Breast. Maidens have breasts and breasts are ..."

"I get ..." Ted tried to speak.

"Basa," Bruce spoke loud. "He does not understand. He must have lived under a rock. Show him a breast."

"Well," Ted said, "if you insist."

"No." Lincoln said. "Stop that." He looked in the rearview mirror.

Basa was standing, her hand on her vest.

"As much as it pains me," Lincoln said. "It's okay, you can put the breasts away."

"I do not mind," she said. "I take great pleasure in educating elders."

"It's fine," Lincoln said. "Ted gets it."

"I get it. I get it," Ted said. "Thank you for the humor, Bruce."

"I have many more."

Bob spoke up. "Let's say ... for shits and giggles ..."

"Shits and giggles?" Bruce asked. "Who wants anything for shits and giggles?"

"Okay," Bob waved his hand. "It's an expression. Let's say Ted is right and all of you are characters from some sort of game who have brought the game to our world. Unknowingly mind you. All of you minded your own business and things started to happen. Now how many times have you done the pattern you told Ted about? Chased the dragons, kill the dragons, rescue burning citizens from villages."

"Enough to get freaking good," Ignatius answered. "We are all Rank Eighteen, the highest in our world. But this is the first time an outside force has taken out the dragons and replacement ones came in. Bruce, how many draconem have we slain?"

Bruce stood up and lifted his shirt.

Ted did a double take. "Are they ... are they carved slash marks in your flesh?"

"They are," Bruce answered proudly. "I have carved them myself. One for each Draco."

Ignatius began counting the slashes, touching each one. As he did, Bruce giggled with each touch. "Forty-eight. So like Eighteen times. A Rank each time. But that's over years. After the next round of three draconem, there will be a small period where nothing happens."

"And, have you noticed each time was different?" Bob asked.

"It seems to get harder, yes," Ignatius replied.

Samuelson spoke up. "His pen of creatures is large and he is always finding new ones to throw our way."

"I have a question," Ted said. "What happens when you die?"

"What happens when we die?" Paxton repeated the question.

"Yes. Die. Killed by a dragon or one of the beasts," Ted explained. "What happens to you?"

"Well, my friend," Paxton answered. "It all depends on what one believes. Some would say you ascend to heavens and live in beauty where your soul is free from worry and pain."

"Or," Ignatius added. "Nothing. You just die."

"Not me!" Bruce said. "When I die, I will go to a plain where I will be greeted and served by a dozen women with bountiful breasts. Breasts, younger sibling. They are ..." Bruce cupped his hands in front of his chest.

"I know what breasts are."

Lincoln glanced at his brother. "Why would you ask that?"

"It's a game," Ted said, "I was wondering what happened when they died. I mean, did they respawn?"

"Like a zombie?" asked Ignatius.

"We have not fought the undead," Bruce said. "I would welcome that."

"No, no, no." Ted shook his head. "I mean as yourself. Like you get another shot. Your life is restored."

"What!" squealed Lincoln. "Ted, this isn't *Jumanji*."

Ignatius laughed. "We don't come back. Do you? I mean if we did have endless lives, we would still have Clausus and Fretator and others that have perished along the way."

Bob shook his head. "And you have never found this Maniacal Master?"

Ignatius shook his head. "No. We think we get close, but we have yet to find his lair."

"So, you haven't even seen him?" Bob questioned.

"Oh! Oh!" Samuelson raised his hand. "I have. He appeared to me in the sky, a huge image and he laughed at me. Ha, ha, ha, ha."

"What did he look like?" Bob asked.

"He was very blue."

Ted looked at Lincoln. "There goes your theory it's some kid in Iowa playing a game."

Lincoln grumbled.

"Has anyone, like a stranger, ever approached you and given you information about him?" Bob asked. "Like randomly would say strange things to you."

"Ha!" Bruce laughed once. "All the time when we leave the villages that we help. They speak in riddles."

"No," Paxton spoke. "They are frightened and know not what they say."

"Wait," Ted said. "Someone comes up to you in every village. Is this before or after they give you weapons?"

"Before," Paxton said. "To one of us. Never all."

"Did someone speak to one of you in Pittsburgh?" Bob questioned.

Paxton pointed to Basa.

"Basa," Bob called to him. "You have been very quiet."

Basa snapped to attention. "My apologies Elderson. I was thinking of battle strategy."

"Did someone say something to you in Pittsburgh right before you guys got the bag of weapons. Some random sentence."

"Oh, yes, as always," Basa said. "Rambling rhyming barbs of a scared citizen. He said something about, forget the plight, the master is not to the right."

"See?" Ignatius said. "It doesn't make sense."

"Actually, it does." Bob pulled the map forward. "I thought it was weird, the pattern of attacks by the dragons. But after marking the cities they hit. First hit was Pittsburgh, then Erie, Cleveland, Columbus, Charleston, Washington, Baltimore, Harrisburg, then Bradford. I marked the map. It makes a circle."

"Yes, it does," Ignatius replied. "It is always the way it is. They create a boundary and fill in everything as the days go on."

Ted asked, "What are you getting at Uncle Bob?"

"Just that. Iggy, did you guys ever pay attention to the random stranger that told you things?"

Ignatius scoffed. "No, it was crazy talk."

"No, it wasn't," Bob said. "If the Maniacal Master set up a territory with the dragons and everything takes place in the circle, then the circle becomes the playing field. Right?" Bob smoothed his hand over the map. "Forget all other clues before they dropped in. Because this is now a new playing field. If this indeed is a game, this big circle is the game board. If you were playing a board game, you wouldn't sit in the middle of the board. Say the message again, Basa."

"Forget the plight, the master is not to the right," Basa stated.

Ted's eyes widened. "He's outside the circle."

"Not to the right," Bob said. "He's out west."

"Guys," Lincoln spoke up. "Hate to interrupt the productive pow-wow, but I think we might be on the right track. We have company ahead."

Ted turned around. A military blockade was on the road ahead.

Lincoln hit the brakes, maybe a little harder than he should have. When he did, Ignatius fell over and rolled to the front between Lincoln and Ted.

"Ow, you were right," Ignatius said. "I should have set down."

ELEVEN

ENCHANTMENT

"What are we looking at?" Ignatius asked as he picked himself up off the floor. He faced out the windshield towards an orange plastic fence set up with several military vehicles, tents, and soldiers holding automatic weapons, keeping guard.

"I shall handle this!" Basa shouted as she opened the van door. "I am eager to join their recruitment or they to ours."

"Oh, they're gonna love you." Lincoln reached for his door handle. "Let's go Ted."

Excitedly, Basa made her way to the men holding weapons. If they were blocking off the way, surely they were close to the draconem? She was well aware, however, they knew very little of what they were up against and they would welcome her expertise and help.

"Greetings my fellow warriors!" Basa said brightly as she approached them.

She knew right then and there that they knew she was needed, they perked with attention and smiled.

"It is with great honor," she said, "that I join your cause, or you join mine in the quest to slay the beasts that reign devastation upon this fair village."

"Huh?" the soldier asked, he shifted his views. "Hey," he spoke to Ted and Lincoln. "You guys can lower your hands, this is just a roadblock."

The brothers lowered their hands and moved closer.

"What a smart move to block the road," Basa said. "We shall pass through to assist in the hunting of the beasts. They slumber now."

"I can't really say anything: except you can't get through here," the soldier said.

"We must."

"You can't."

"I need to speak to your general then, the leader of your fine hunting team."

"Um ..." The soldier looked to his left. "Sarge!"

Another soldier came over, he seemed slightly annoyed. The name Gilmore was on the tag above his pocket.

"What is the issue here." He saw Basa and smiled. "Can I help you ma'am?"

"My great general. We need to get by."

"I'm sure you think that," he replied. "Considering this road doesn't lead to any towns. Farmington is back there." He pointed. "There's no reason for you to get through."

"Ah, but you are wrong," said Basa. "We are warriors here to slay the draconem."

"How about that?" Gilmore said. "So are we." He looked at Ted. "Can you take your friend away from here please, thank you."

Feeling helpless at what to do or even what move to make, Ted turned slightly to Lincoln. "There has to be another way."

"Here comes Ignatius. He'll get us through."

Ted spoke though clenched jaws. "Hope he doesn't transform us into a dragon again."

Ignatius walked up to Basa. "Come on. Let's go. Back to the van."

"We are not giving up," said Basa. "I must insist you let us through, Good leader of warriors. We fight the same battle, yet you know not what you face."

"I kinda think we do. And ..." Gilmore groaned. "Can anyone else get out of the van? People, you need to turn around."

Bruce walked forward. "Slay the draconem!"

Ted planted a face palm. "Oh. My. God." He slid his fingers across his face. "Guys, come on."

"Listen to your friend," Gilmore said. "Don't make me get angry."

"Angry?" Basa asked. "Get angry at the beasts that rest behind the forest line. Allow us to pass and do what we came to do. You have never faced such beasts."

"And you have?"

"Bruce! Show the warrior leader."

Bruce lifted his shirt. "Mark for each dragon kill."

"Oh. My. God," Lincoln rushed forward. "Enough guys, I'm sure Ignatius will find away."

"I will," said Ignatius. "Not this way. Basalous, come."

Basa ignored Ignatius. "They do not understand the perils they face. The Maniacal Master places many dangers ahead of the beasts, it is not as easy as walking up to them and slitting their bellies."

"The Maniacal Master, huh?" Gilmore said snidely.

"He is crafty," said Basa. "He will throw many obstacles at you. Like bunnies and unicorns."

"Bunnies and unicorns. Oh, wow, thanks for the heads up."

"And trolls."

"Yeah, they can be bad. Now leave now or I will detain you," Gilmore ordered.

"Detain us? We are your best hope. You think you can slay them. Do you have weapons like this ..." Basa drew her fiery swords.

Along with a, "whoa, whoa, whoa," from Gilmore came the sound of the soldiers raising and arming their weapons.

Basa scoffed. "Yes, those will work," she said totally oblivious to the fact that they were aimed at her. "We have more of those weapons in our transport."

Ted cringed. "We're screwed."

Gilmore kept his aim on Basa. "Waites. Go check that van."

The other soldier, Waites, walked quickly to the van.

"We will gladly share what we have. We will walk along with you. I will teach you the secrets of …"

"Sarge!" Waites called out. "Looks like we have some contraband."

Lincoln spoke low to Ted. "About this time, someone has to do something."

"Um, not me."

Gilmore growled loudly. "Is there anyone else!" he shouted. "That wants to come out of that van? Waites, find the sheriff, he's back at the tent."

As if he were taking a leisurely stroll, Paxton, with a tilted head and a smile, walked to Gilmore.

"My good, sir," said Paxton. "I understand this is frustrating for you. I will retreat my comrades."

"Not gonna happen," Gilmore said. "Not now. You had your chance."

"May I just draw your attention for a moment?" Paxton asked. "Look at me. Do I look threatening?"

Gilmore looked at Paxton, and he seemed just slightly for a moment to freeze. "Wow," he said to Paxton. "Did anyone ever tell you that you have fantastic eyes."

"All the time." Paxton grinned. "May we pass through to slay the dragon? We are authorized to be here by your state authorities."

"You can do anything you want." Gilmore whistled to Waites. "Shut the van hatch. We're letting them through. They're allowed. They're gonna slay the dragons."

"Whatever you say, Sarge," Waites replied.

"Thank you," Paxton said. He turned with hands behind his back, gave a nod to Basa, Ignatius and the brothers, then walked back toward the van. "Lincoln let us go."

Lincoln exhaled loudly. "That was weird."

"Tell me about it. Would have been cooler with Basa," Ted said. "I see how it's helpful now."

"He's a Prince." Lincoln walked back to the van. "You know they only had him come along because of that. How else is he going to use that skill? Enchant a dragon?"

"Oh my God," Ted laughed. "That would be like Donkey in *Shrek*."

They both got another laugh out of the Sergeant staring amorously as he watched Paxton walk away.

It was a strange way to get through the barricade, but at least they were getting through.

TWELVE

SCOUR

There were too many mountain ranges and too much forestry in the tristate area of Pennsylvania, West Virginia and Maryland to count. The intuitive guidance of Samuelson led them to the wooded and cavernous area south of the City of Pittsburgh. Close enough to where they left Bea, Sally and Officer Bill Smith, that they'd return to them in the morning to rest for whatever battle remained.

While Ted, Lincoln and the Portal Five followed an 'out worldly' guidance, the military followed radar, but locals from a neighboring small town watched the sky and saw the dragons disappear into the trees.

All of them ended up in the same place.

It felt to Ted like some sort of scavenger hunt competition, groups spreading out, no one sharing information, no one listening to Basa, who finally shut up after the first two hours.

It was dark, really dark. The smoke from the rash of recent fires from the dragons blocked out the stars and moon. Those in

113

the military search party had flashlights and night vision. The locals carried spotlights.

Ted's group carried torches, looking like they were on some lynch mob hunt for Frankenstein.

"Why at night?" Ted asked. "Do they tire?"

Samuelson answered. "Yes and no. The retreat mainly at night because they cannot see very well in the dark and direct light into their eyes blinds them. They do tire, but do not let that fool you. They are still very strong. Angry when woken."

"Oh, I get that," Ted replied. "If I don't want to get up, I'm horrible."

"Samuelson," Lincoln called for his attention. "There are a lot of caves around here. Do you think they might be there?"

"No," Samuelson replied. "When they retreat to a cave it is because they seek safety during the day, which is not a consideration for them in this world. It only happens when something has frightened them."

"Like what?" Ted asked. "They're dragons."

"Another dragon," Samuelson said. "There are bigger ones than these. Only the larger ones cannot fly as long and they are not fire breathing."

"That's good to know." Ted looked at Lincoln. "We couldn't get those ones. No, we got the ones that destroy everything."

"We got the ones that are most depicted in games and books," said Lincoln.

"So, you believe me now about it being a game?"

"I never said I didn't. I'm just saying when that portal opened some sort of weird world collided with ours. I hope you're right, Ted. I do. If it's a game, like Uncle Bob said. There's an end game and we'll figure out how to get there. Just, you know, too bad we couldn't go online and get cheats like we did when we couldn't conquer *Way Dead*."

Ted stopped walking.

"What is it?"

"Nothing. Just a thought." Ted shook his head.

"Shh," Ignatius told them.

"You can't get cheats for a game that's not readily available. If that's what you're thinking. Remember when we clicked on it, it said we were first."

"True."

"Shh."

"Oh," Ted snapped a little. "Shh, yourself."

"You okay?" Lincoln asked.

"Yeah, just thinking about Mom, worried about her and Aunt Sally."

"They're with Officer Bill Smith. They're fine and by the time he leaves to get his gram," Lincoln said. "We'll be back."

"Shh."

"Oh my God," Lincoln whispered harshly. "We know! This isn't a library."

Ignatius spun around. "Keep talking. Go on. When they come out of the woods and bite your brother's head off then you'll be like, 'oh, no I should have listened to Iggy.'"

"Really?" Lincoln asked. "Bite my brother's head off."

"Why *my* head?" Ted asked. "Why not his?"

"Shh."

"Fine." Ted shook his head, then touched it.

They moved slowly, keeping talk to a minimum and soft. The soldier and the local men that came in search of the dragons were also quiet. Ted only could see their lights dancing as the search parties moved through the woods and up the hill.

A distance separated them all. Each group at least fifty yards from the next.

"I smell them," Bruce announced quietly. "Soon you will, too."

Ted didn't know why, but hearing Bruce say that sent a shiver up his neck. It was a cool, dense night, with air that felt thick and Ted tried to see if he could catch a scent, as well.

"Watch where you walk," said Bruce.

Crunch.

Ted looked sharply to his right. "What was that?"

"Uh," Bob stammered, lifting his leg and shaking it. "I stepped on something. I don't know what it is. I can't see. I think it's a dead animal or something."

Ted and Lincoln stayed behind Ignatius as he brought the torch to where Uncle Bob stood.

When he brought the torch down to lighten the area, the orange hue of the flame illuminated a human head. The remains of the body were torn apart, as if eaten.

Bob shrieked, turned and immediately vomited.

Ted wanted to vomit as well, but when he stepped back, he felt a painful pinch to his ankle. "Ow. Shit. Something bit me."

Lincoln looked over to him. "Was it a ... ow. Ow." He jumped back.

A distance cry of a man in pain echoed through the woods.

"I can't see it," Ted said rushed and panicked. "It keeps biting me."

Bruce glanced over his shoulder, and Ted saw the look on his face. "Bunnies," Bruce said with deep seriousness.

"Bunnies?" Ted questioned with a cracking voice. "How can they be ..." His eyes widened and he glanced down. Even in the dark he could see the black furry creature crawling up his leg. Its ears were long and floppy like a rabbit. Its paws were claw like as it clutched to Ted's jeans. And the usual cute little nibbling teeth were replaced with tusk like fangs.

Ted grabbed on to it before it could bite him. The animal wiggled violently in his grip, and all Ted could think to do was throw it.

Ignatius spun with his torch like a baseball player, nipping the creature with the flame, causing it to squeal loudly.

Another cry out came from the forest, then another. It was either some serious killer bunnies or something else. Whatever caused it was picking the other teams off, one by one.

"The bunnies are hurrying away," said Paxton.

And with those words, Bruce ordered, "Run!"

"Where?" Ted asked.

"Away from the screams," Lincoln said.

Ted and Lincoln rushed off, following behind the others, as Bruce led the way.

They hadn't made it far when they heard the cracking of trees, along with tromping and crunching.

"I thought they couldn't see in the dark," Ted panted as he ran.

"They're following our scent and sound," Ignatius said. "I told you to be quiet."

"Don't put this one us!" Ted yelled.

Then, suddenly, a loud, blasting roar stopped them all in their tracks.

Quiet.

An insane silence

Slowly, Bruce lifted his torch.

The eyes of the beast were right there. They were large, bigger than a human skull. The dragon, startled by the light, cocked back its head and roared. A roar so mighty it blasted them all with a foul-smelling air.

"Basalous!" Bruce called out, dropped the torch, and jumped onto the beast. He moved fast for a man of his size, one hand grabbing on to the rugged flesh of the drag's neck, using it as leverage to climb on to its back.

Bruce's large hands looked like baby hands against the jaw of the dragon, but he managed to push the bottom jaw closed. After he did that, he secured his arms around the mouth of the dragon, keeping it tight.

While the beast struggled and arched its neck, Basa, with swords aflame, raced forward, jumped up, and with one mighty, horizontal swing, slit the beast's neck.

"Free the souls!" Bruce cried out. "Now while I have him."

The monster still struggled, though not as violently, as blood poured from its neck. While it was still in the upright position, Basa used her other sword, cutting upward through the hide in an instant gutting of the beasts.

Like a broken pinata the contents of its belly poured out. Only it wasn't candy. It was remains of people and animals.

Ted was so hypnotized with shock by the sight of it, he never heard what was happening behind him.

"Ted! Watch out!" Uncle Bob yelled.

Lincoln grabbed Ted's arm, yanking him hard out of the way. As he turned, he saw the other dragon had been standing right behind him.

Before he could even panic, or get his legs to move, the 'rat-tat-tat' of the automatic rifle rang out, as Uncle Bob unloaded on the beast.

The ex-Marine stepped close. Making sure each shot wasn't random, he aimed for the head, but the dragon kept trying to snap out and bite, so the shots landed on its neck.

Each hit caused blood to squirt out until the multiple hits caused the flesh on the neck of the beast to rip apart. Its legs weakened and finally it fell to the ground. It was pathetic and fatally injured. Its wings flapping in some sort of dying twitch. Uncle Bob didn't stop shooting until Paxton approached, jamming his sword into the eye of the dragon, sealing its fate with death.

Ted didn't know what to say: he wanted to thank Uncle Bob, because if it hadn't been for him Ted would have been killed.

"You alright?" Lincoln asked him. "Bro that was so close. I thought Ignatius was gonna be right."

"It almost bit my head off, didn't it?"

"Yeah."

"Uncle Bob was cool," Ted said and walked to his Uncle who stood staring at the body of the dragon. He started to say something, but a slow, unfamiliar, deep voice echoed through thin air.

"The Elderson Warrior. Rank Two achieved."

Ted looked around. "Who said that?"

"Unbelievable," Lincoln replied looking up into the darkness for the source.

Then a steady and heavy clapping came from Bruce.

"There." Lincoln pointed. "Freaking Bruce throwing his voice or something."

"Nothing like him bro'. That was a game message," Ted replied.

"You are a Warrior. Well done my friend." Bruce approached, slapping Bob on the back sending him a stumbling forward. "Well done indeed. The gods have granted you this. What an honor. Now when you face the beast again, those weapons will yield far more power than they did today."

"Thanks," Uncle Bob said. "But I don't think it works that way. The rifles won't get any more powerful."

"Oh, but *you* will. You heard the gods speak in the wind," Bruce said.

Samuelson added. "When the gods speak and reward you, it is a great privilege."

"You should be joyed," said Basa. "I recall the day when a butcher was named The Butcher by the gods. His hatchet could then slice a stone."

"What a great man." Bruce lowered his head.

"His loss will be felt for all times," added Basa.

"And so should yours," Bruce told Uncle Bob. "Should you now die in battle."

"That's good to know."

"And now…" Bruce reached out and pulled the sword from the dragon's eye. He handed it to Uncle Bob. "You shall have the honor of freeing the souls."

"I'm not sure how to do that," Uncle Bob said. "Why don't you do it?"

121

"I will do it in your honor."

"Hey, Bruce," Ted called out. "Can you not …"

Ted cringed at the sound as Bruce gutted the dragon in one stroke. He heard the contents pour out and hit the ground and Ted was grateful it was dark, because he didn't have to see it.

THIRTEEN

CHANGE UP

They never heard it. Had Officer Bill Smith not shown up and decided to stay outside, Bea and Sally certainly would have died.

He heard the distant howling screeches. The same ones he had heard the day before when he was downtown Pittsburgh.

They both were sound asleep when he raced into the camper, shouted for them to get up and buckle in, as he jumped in the driver's seat and took off from their spot.

"Grab what you can. Water, food, guns. Grab it. Also blankets."

"What's happening?" Bea asked, making her way to the front. She held on with each step because Office Bill Smith drove like a mad man.

"They're coming."

"Who?"

"You mean 'what'," said Officer Bill Smith. "The dragons."

"What?" Sally asked in shock as she shoved things in a bag. "The Wizard said this was safe. We're out in the middle of nowhere."

"I just know what I heard and it didn't sound good," he replied.

The road wasn't designed for a large vehicle to barrel down.

"Where are we headed?" Bea asked.

"Deep in the woods; conceal ourselves."

"Do you really think they'll hit here? Maybe they were somewhere else?" Bea suggested.

The second she said that, a huge blast of fire struck the road and had Officer Bill Smith not jerked the wheel hard to the left in a nick of time, the explosion of flames would have engulfed them.

He veered the camper down a hillside and across a picnic area. His sights were set on the line of trees in the distance.

He didn't know how many dragons were out there, but he could see two, both swooping down.

"Will we fit in the trees?" Bea asked.

"No," he replied. "We won't."

"What are we gonna do."

"I'm gonna get us there, pull as close as I can, swing this bad boy around sideways. I need you two by that side door now. Go," he instructed. "Open it and when I stop, run out as fast as you can through the woods."

"I'm not finished grabbing things," said Sally.

"I don't care. Go!" Officer Bill Smith said. "When you get out, just run."

He lifted his sight to the rearview mirror. His foot pressed the pedal all the way to the floor as he swerved the camper left and right trying to avoid the torpedo shots of fire.

How they didn't roll he didn't know.

The tree line was close. Almost there.

"Hold on!" he yelled out. Just as he arrived at the tree line, he turned the wheel, sending the camper in a spin.

Officer Bill Smith jumped from his seat, ran to the back and leapt from the open side door. He hit the ground by the edge of the streets, rolling into the weeds, as the dragons fired down at the camper then flew off.

The camper was consumed by flames instantaneously, and, as if they were making sure they had hit their targets, both dragons made another pass, blasting it again.

He watched, only a few feet from the camper. He could feel the heat of the fire. Then he felt both his arms being grabbed.

"Come on," Bea said. "Let's go" She tugged him.

"Wait," Office Bill Smith said, "I don't think they're coming back."

"Were they targeting us?" Bea asked.

"I don't know."

He stood and brushed himself off.

"Jesus," Sally gasped out, stepping forward. "Look at them."

At that point, Officer Bill Smith noticed there were four dragons. They flew off, no distinct pattern, playfully swooping around each other as they randomly spat fire below.

Why had they deliberately destroyed the van? If, indeed, that was what the dragons were doing.

The blasts of flames from the dragons sparked sporadic fires in the direction they had to take.

"How far are we?" Sally asked.

"I don't know. Not that far from where we were," he answered. "But we need to move now."

"How?" Sally asked.

"Well, it's called Mingo Creek Park. Let's find that creek," Officer Bill Smith said. "We'll follow that."

The camper was an inferno and they avoided that as they moved forward.

Office Bill Smith wasn't an expert on forest fires, but he was smart enough to know that with the way the flames were growing, if they didn't get out of the park fast, they were never getting out of the place.

<><><><><>

The intention was to get back to Mingo and the camper before dawn, but that didn't happen. The Portal Five along with Uncle Bob took down the dragons. Ted was still in shock, processing the entire situation.

How brave they all were. None of them, Bruce, Basa, Paxton, and even Uncle Bob, hesitated in doing what they had to do.

But even after slaying the dragons, there was more work to be done.

There were injured men throughout the hillside and forest that needed help.

The bunny attack was vicious, some men were overcome by dozens of them. Gnawed upon in bits and pieces until they died.

They spent the remainder of the night, helping the injured to the medical tents.

Even Ted needed a bandage. The bite he sustained on the leg was deep. A medic gave him a shot of antibiotics and a topical for the pain. It wasn't deep enough to get stitches.

When dawn broke, they were ready to leave. They wanted to go to Mingo, but were asked to stay, just a little bit longer until Colonel Hanson arrived.

Ted didn't understand why. He didn't know how to explain to the game characters that they were requested to wait. He figured they were in some sort of trouble with the authorities, even though everyone kept telling them how good of a job they did.

Was it really?

In the end, twelve men lost their lives and another eight were injured.

Sergeant Gilmore kept Ted, Lincoln and the Portal Five in a separate tent while waiting on the Colonel.

In every story, movie or even game, if a dragon was slain, there was no follow up. Everyone just moved on to the next adventure or lived happily ever after. Here, this was not the case, and Ted learned that when the colonel showed up.

"Gentlemen," The colonel said when he walked into the tent. "And lady." He made a point of shaking everyone's hand as he spoke. "I am told that without you …" He paused at Samuelson. "Anyone ever tell you that you look just like Sam Elliott?"

"Yes, and my name is Sam."

"Look at that." He shook Bruce's hand. "You must be the guy that wrestles them?"

"I break them. Then we slay them." He lifted his shirt and exposed his slashes, one of them were fresh and bleeding. "I mark my body for the draconem we slay."

"Why is there only one bleeding and new one. I thought you killed two?" Colonel Hanson asked.

"I took down one with Basalous. Warrior Elderson Bob, took down the other." Bruce lifted his knife. "Uncle Bob you should let me mark your flesh for the kill."

"No, that's okay," Bob said.

"Be proud."

"I'm fine."

"Your woman will give herself to you when she sees the mark of your bravery."

"You know what?" Bob said. "Sure. Go on." He lifted his shirt.

The colonel smiled. "I don't know where you men and lady have learned about dragons. But I am impressed and grateful. I …" He paused when Bob let out a stifled scream of pain. "As I was saying …" he watched Bruce firmly pat Bob on the shoulder. "I don't know what one of you having fantastic eyes has to do with anything, but those eyes got you in and I am glad. Right now, we need to know everything you know."

Samuelson widened his arms. "We are a vat upon which you may tap."

"Good. Good," said the Colonel. "Let's start by going up that hill and you show me those dragons."

Ted wanted to refuse. Never in his imagination did he envision a follow up to the slaying of dragons. Even the Portal Five never mentioned going back to where the dragon carcasses lay.

He did, however, speak up to tell the colonel that they had to get back home. They had people waiting and they were worried. Colonel Hanson assured them they wouldn't be long.

"What's the issue?" Lincoln asked Ted.

"I don't want to go back up there. The dragons are dead. We move on."

"Yeah, but you're the one convinced it's a game, right?" Lincoln said. "It may not have been burnt villagers, but we helped a lot of people last night."

"Okay. What's that have to do with going back up there?"

"It's all part of the pattern, maybe some random person will give us a clue."

"And another bag of weapons."

"That's possible. It's worth a shot. Obviously, our portal friends never paid attention to the clues. That's where we come in. So we go up, just in case. Besides," Lincoln added, "they're dead. How bad can it be?"

<><><><><><>

What he saw in the dark, needed to stay in the dark. The morning sun brightened more than the sky, it lit up the horrors of night before. Body parts strewn about the forest, guts hung from trees, and the contents of the dragon's belly revealed.

The monsters had consumed more than Ted would have imagined, people and animals, some in half, some whole. They were covered with a thick, green, stomach acid that sizzled and ate away the flesh.

"We thought," Hanson said, "maybe you guys were a joke. Apparently, from what my lot say, you are far from that. I don't know where you came from. I don't want to know. We have a problem that you can help solve. Can you tell me why you gut them? Is it a way to make sure they're dead?"

Samuelson shook his head. "It is a way to release the spirits of those the beasts consumed."

"What do you know about dragon behavior?" Hanson asked. "Other than using fire and eating people. How often do they adapt to their surroundings?"

Lincoln asked, "What do you mean?"

"I mean, they're smart, but it's strange. When the first ones arrived, we took them out, piece of cake. The second wave of them proved a bit more challenging, still our jets got them. These two … they managed to avoid our best fighter pilots. But the ones this morning, after they started blasting areas again … they seemed to be waiting for our planes. And the dragons, they took them out. They took down our jets. Like they're all operating on one brain, nesting somewhere."

Ignatius shook his head. "That's not the way it works. There's no large gathering or nests. They just come in their pairs or groups."

"I'm sorry … are they …" Hanson pointed. "Do you have … wings?"

"I do and they are, I'm a Fairy. And he …" Ignatius pointed to Samuelson. "Is a Wizard. He is a Prince, and she …" He swung his point to Basa. "Is a Slayer."

"I am a Barbarian," said Bruce. "And forget not the Warrior." He pointed to Uncle Bob.

"And …" Hanson faced Lincoln and Ted. "You two?"

Ted answered. "Just two brothers that got caught up in all this."

With a straight face, Ignatius said, "that one has a high skill in soap opera knowledge."

"There's an old saying my mother used to say to me," Hanson said. "Birds of a feather flock together, but you're saying the dragons don't. Are they creatures of habit? I mean, they have to have some sort of pattern if you men know them so well that you can take them down with ease."

131

"They're very pattern oriented," Ignatius said. "They hit all the targets they want to, then they will make a second pass and hit them again. It's like a dinner plate. The area they hit, they will keep getting it until it's clean, or in this case … destroyed."

"And they don't nest together?" Hanson asked. "These two you killed were not the ones that destroyed everything yesterday. But they're following the same pattern?"

Ignatius nodded. "They do. Strike, rest, strike again. Unless we take them down."

"But you killed these two," Hanson said. "And we killed the others so, if they aren't all part of one big dragon network, then how did the four this morning know to finish the job and to get the jets."

"Wait, did you say four?" Ignatius asked.

"Yes."

"That's impossible. Never in all the ones we chased have there been more than three."

"There were four, son, and they didn't go on to another city, they seemed to retreat east. Like the first ones, to Butler Knob."

"They retreated and went to the mountains?" Ignatius asked.

"They did."

"In the daylight?"

"That's why I wanted to talk to you. We have them on scanners. We have eyes on them. We want to get you and your … Wizard, Barbarian and killer …"

"Slayer," Basa corrected.

"Yes," said Hanson. "Have your team come east. We're hoping it's a reprieve and we are trying to evacuate everyone we can and move them west. The attacks seem to be focused in one wide area like you said. The rest of the country is fine."

Ted saw it on Ignatius face: utter confusion over what the colonel was saying. Ted understood. Ignatius and the rest of the Portal Five knew the pattern of the dragons well and the report from the colonel was clearly something Ignatius didn't expect.

Ted did.

The Maniacal Master or whoever was running the game, had upped the anti and the game was about to get harder. It would be too easy to stay on top of the challenges if they knew the next move.

The colonel was asking them to go east, Ted assumed, to help track and take down the dragons. Which in real life made no sense. The military didn't need the Portal Five. Not with all their technology. But in a controlled game, new quests like that were available after the ending of an old one.

The mysterious man giving a clue.

A bag of weapons just left behind.

Without a doubt the game-world they were now living in was being controlled. As were the dragons.

While Ted's mind was going to the game and what could happen, Lincoln spoke up. "Colonel, you said they hit and didn't continue on. That they went east. Where did they hit this morning?"

"Pittsburgh again," Hanson answered. "And they pummelled south of the city. It was strange, they hit low population areas. Like it was some sort of coordinated attack."

When Ted heard that, it clicked in him. Was it coordinated or calculated? The Maniacal Master was one step ahead of them. Changing patterns, knowing the jets would attack. Then there was how easily and quietly the dragons had taken out so many men in the forest the night before.

In Ted's mind, the retreat to the east was nothing less than a set up.

Samuelson was right. As impossible as it seemed, the Maniacal Master was in control. But how? How was he doing it? Almost as if he were some sort of god looking down.

All those thoughts and going east would have to wait.

After hearing where the dragons attacked, all Ted could think of was his mother and Aunt Sally: they were south of the city. Before helping the colonel and going east, they had to go back to find his family.

FOURTEEN

TIMBER

They were fifty-five miles southeast of Mingo Creek County Park. During their journey north to get there, they saw the massive exodus movement going south.

The four-lane road was converted to three lanes all going south. They drove behind a military truck headed toward Pittsburgh, otherwise, they would be prohibited from traveling that way.

All civilians were.

The emergency alert system was activated, alerting all civilians in the Pittsburgh area to head south west as far as they could go.

Ted heard them spew forth from areas that were designated for refugees, but he didn't listen, he was too focused on going between watching his phone for a signal and looking at the thick line of traffic moving at a crawling pace.

A huge target should the dragons return.

All Ted kept thinking was, even if they were part of a game, the loss of lives, the destruction, the fear ... that was real.

Just the day before his brother was working as if everything was normal. In actuality, it wasn't, bad things just hadn't started yet.

Still too far to even see the city skyline, the sky in the distance was pink.

Lincoln's face read like a first grade book. Too easy to not know what he was feeling or thinking. Then again, they were so close as brothers, most of the time Ted knew what Lincoln was going to do.

"This is screwed up," Lincoln said. "Everyone we know, I can't stop thinking about them. Our friends."

"Makes me glad I never had a kid."

"Yeah, me, too." Lincoln looked at Ted. "This isn't going to go away after we beat this Maniacal Master or whatever."

"We don't know that. I mean, when we beat him, things might all go back."

"Can we beat him?"

"Yes, we just don't know how."

"Honestly, Ted. If this is some sort of game, I can see us hitting a boss fight where everything is thrown at us." Lincoln looked into the rearview mirror. "And why are they all so quiet."

"We're thinking," Ignatius spoke up. "At least I am. We have not been in this position. It's always been the exact same way. Throw some bunnies, some obstacles, like last night, yes. But they slammed one area and retreated."

"You said they usually hit a place over and over until it's completely destroyed," Ted said. "That's what you told us."

"Yes," Ignatius replied.

"So, I take it you have seen an area demolished?" Lincoln asked.

"We have. The dragons had hit every town and village within the circle they'd set," Ignatius explained. "We thought that they would just move on to another area, like on the other side of the mountains or sea. Maniacal Master picked another area. He brought us here."

"No," Samuelson said. "The brothers brought us here. They opened the portal. Yes, the Maniacal Master created the portal. But, they tapped into whatever magic the Maniacal Master uses. If they hadn't, we'd still be battling on the other side."

"But would you have?" Ted asked. "You completed a big quest. You're here for the next battle. Did you by chance look back at all to see if everything was still destroyed, considering finished in that world, did it revert back?"

"We were brought through," Samuelson said. "I did not see if it reverted back. Again, something you two did brought us through."

Ted looked at Lincoln. "When we clicked on the new instance on the computer, the one no one else had played, for us, that new game is what's happening now. Can't you see that Link?"

Samuelson asked. "Can you use that computer somehow to save your villages?"

"If only. Because trust me, it would be over if it we could." Lincoln shook his head. "I don't know. Right now, we don't have

137

access to anything. In this area the dragons have destroyed everything. We'd have to leave the circle of destruction to find a computer and get online. Even then, I don't know what we'd see when we log-in to the game."

"It has to be connected," Ted said.

"Four," Basa spoke up. "Why four this time? In all the times we battled the dragons never have there been four."

"Because," Ted answered. "You know how to do it. You know how to beat two or three. It changed up to make it harder."

"He wants you at the next rank, or whatever," Uncle Bob interjected. "He's pushing you. You guys never picked up on the clues on where he was or how to get him. If there is a master guy controlling this, he's getting tired of you guys just running in circles so he's leading you with something."

"We helped in the woods," Ted said. "All those injured. Why wasn't there a magic bag of weapons or a random clue said by someone?"

"There was," Uncle Bob said. "The whole situation. The clue was the Colonel asking a Fairy, Slayer, Prince, Barbarian, Wizard, middle-aged man and two under-achieving thirty-something brothers to lead the dragon attack. That's odd. That should never have happened. The weapon bag is what the United States Army has at its disposal."

"You believe we're in a game then?" asked Ted.

"What else makes any sense? And after that voice in the sky. Well, I feel young again. I bet I could hit a bullseye every time."

"Right. You ranked up."

"It seems to me though, if the whole shebang is the current party quest," Bob said, "there's not much further the game can go."

Ted nodded, "Yeah. But does it feel like we're on the last ever quest? It can't be."

"Maybe it's the penultimate one," Uncle Bob said. "I have played games where the next-to-last fight was the hardest."

"I don't know." Ted sat back. "I feel like we're missing something. That something is going to click and we're gonna all have that 'oh, yeah' moment. What do you think, Link?"

Lincoln hesitated before answering. "Thirty-something under-achiever?"

"Seriously?" Ted asked. "We're talking here about everything that's going on and you bring up that?"

"Yes, yes, I do. That pisses me off. I have spent the last five years of my life getting out of the musician rut. Realizing I can still play music and have a job. I know, I know, it's the big joke. I manage Arby's. I'm a general manager. I make good money and bonuses. No offence Uncle Bob, but under-achiever? I can see you saying that about Ted."

"Hey."

"No, not hey," Lincoln said. "You had your life together, a good job... a house. You owned a house. What happens? Your wife leaves you and you say fuck life. You give her the house, quit your job ..."

"I didn't quit my job, I was fired because she was having an affair with my boss," Ted defended himself.

"You were fired because you stormed into his meeting and clocked the guy," Lincoln said. "Still, you could have had another job, and the house. No. You moved into moms, ate pizza, smoked weed, played games and got addicted to soap operas."

"In his defense," Samuelson broken in, "soap operas are entertaining."

"He could have been addicted to them and had a life," Lincoln said. "Bottom line, he gave up. You gave up, Ted."

"You're right," Ted replied. "You're right. I don't do anything. I live the life of a teenager with a job. I get it. I suck."

"No!" Bruce called out. "You do not … suck. I, too, was where you were. I gave up. My wife left me for a man that makes shoes and has no muscle. No bravery. Shoes. I gave up. I had the drink until I could not stand up. Nightly. Ask Ignatius."

"Oh, yeah, he was bad."

"Then the dragons came, the Maniacal Master came. I found purpose. Now, I will never give up. Like you, Ted. You too now have found the dragons. You now have to fight the Maniacal Master, you … will never give up. I believe in you. Just like Ignatius believed in me."

"Wow." Ted said shocked. "That was like, really deep coming from you Bruce."

"Thank you. When we are done. When the Maniacal Master is defeated," Bruce said. "We will celebrate. We will indulge in

140

drink, wild women and you will let me place the slashes on your stomach."

"Deal," Ted said. "Thanks, Bruce. I mean it."

Bruce nodded. "We are close to that end. I feel it."

"That's not all we're close to," Lincoln said.

After exiting the highway and turning on to a state road, the revelation of how far the dragons had taken the destruction was clear.

They weren't cities, they were small communities that ran alongside the Monongahela River. House, small business, all burning. The dragons had scorched everything in their path.

Very few cars moved on the road, but there were people. Lots of people walking, carrying what they could in their arms. The faces darkened with soot; their eyes lost. Children, holding hands with parents, looked destitute.

Ted wanted his brother to stop, to help the people, but there was nothing they could do, they had to keep moving. They had to find their mom and aunt and head east before sundown.

The tone in the van became solemn and Lincoln turned the wheel, making a right down another state road that would take them to the park entrance.

Four miles. That was all they were from the road that turned into the park. At first, after they turned, things seemed better. Trees were green, no flames. It seemed as if the dragons followed the river. But the farther they drove and nearer to the park, it was abundantly clear, something had happened ahead.

Thick smoke flowed into the sky, darkening it; the smell of 'burning' seeped into the vents of the van. Lincoln drove faster.

After the sharp bend that brought them under the Joe Montana bridge, the flames in the park were seen. They shot up high in the distance.

Though they hadn't reached the road, it was clear, the park had been hit.

Lincoln made the hard turn into the park. The entrance was fire free and he never slowed down. "They're two miles in. They're fine. Or they got out."

At the 'Y' in the road, Lincoln went left. They weren't far, not at all, but he slowed down.

Directly ahead where the trees thickened against the road, everything was ablaze, like one of those documentaries or newsreels about wildfires. Flames snapped and popped, entire trees looking like matchsticks burning.

"Sam," Lincoln called to him. "Can you use your 'know all'? Can you see them."

"Give me a moment," Samuelson said.

Lincoln stopped driving to look back.

Samuelson smoothed his hand over the table. "I see them. They are together. On foot. All three." He peered up. "Flames are on both side of them. They walk in water."

Ted looked at Lincoln. 'The creek."

Immediately, Lincoln threw the van in reverse and backed up hastily until he reached a small clearing where there was a half circle turn around. Using it, Lincoln turned the van for a quick exit.

"Uncle Bob, stay here with the others in case the dragons come back and you have to drive. Ted and I will take the creek." He opened his door and got out.

Ted stepped from the van as well, and so did Bruce and Ignatius.

"We're coming with you two," said Ignatius. "Bruce can help and I can manifest if needed."

Lincoln and Ted led the way, down the slight grade, across the grass and down to the creek. There, the four of them began a fast-paced trek up the water's edge.

Sally coughed. She soaked her sweater in the water and kept it close to her face, but it didn't help. At first it was easy. They had made it to the creek, free of fire and threat of dragons. They walked quickly, staying to the side of the flowing water. The open area around the creek narrowed and the creek wound through a dense wooded area.

Not far into that portion, they saw the fire. There was no turning back, they could only go forward.

Nearly clinging to each other, they stayed in the water that came only to their shins, slipping on the moss-covered stones, and trying to stay focused and moving.

They were surrounded.

The heat intensified, along with the smoke and flames.

No one said anything, fearful of talking, taking as few breaths as possible.

The situation was dire and seemed hopeless. Until, through the orange smoke and glow of the flames, Sally saw them.

"Look. Look." She pointed. "Up ahead."

Bea let out an exhausted sigh of relief.

"A little more," Officer Bill Smith said. "A little more." He held on to both of them, moving them forward.

"Mom, Aunt Sally!" Ted called out. "I see them."

It seemed impossible that they were still standing, let alone moving with the flames so high on both sides of them. He had nearly given up hope when he, Ted, Ignatius and Bruce were no longer in a fire free zone. Flames from ahead were spreading quickly.

But it was over. They found them,

His mom, Aunt and Officer Bill Smith were no more than fifty feet ahead and picking up speed.

Then crash.

From the bank next to the creek came a burning tree. It slammed hard to the ground and over the creek sending embers flying everywhere as sparks.

It still wasn't hopeless. It would be difficult, but the three of them could make it around that tree if they hurried. It was possible. Until another tree fell.

So close.

The double stack of flaming timber separated the brothers from their family.

Ted could see his mother's face, his aunt's. Neither of them looked scared or were showing it.

Through the rippling waves of heat, Ted only saw bravery.

Maybe it was a front they put on as they tried to make eye contact.

"No! No!" Ted ran forward, and a split second later, so did Lincoln.

They didn't make it far, Bruce barrelled forth, pushing between them and shoving them aside as he rushed ahead. He stopped momentarily at the enormous burning tree, then he crouched down, extended his hands into the fire and lifted the tree, hoisting it to the side with apparent ease.

"Bruce!" Ignatius screamed.

Bruce repeated his actions with the other tree, tossing that to the side as well. He never stopped or hesitated. He didn't flinch or cry out in pain when reaching for the burning trees. There was no reaction of anguish even as his clothes caught fire and his skin blackened.

Ted and Lincoln ran forward as Bea, Sandy and Officer Bill Smith emerged into a safer area.

"Get them out," Ted told Officer Bill Smith as he and Lincoln raced to help Bruce. They led led him to the creek and took off their shirts to put out the flames on Bruce's body.

It was heart wrenching. Overwhelmed with relief for his family, yet Ted felt gutted when he saw the damage to Bruce.

It was inconceivable that someone could be so brave and selfless.

Was it a groan, Ted heard from Bruce? He didn't know. But Bruce was still breathing.

"We can carry him," Ted said to Lincoln.

"Yeah, we need to be careful. He's hurt bad." Lincoln crouched down closer. "Hey, Buddy we're gonna help you."

"Ignatius," Ted called. "Can you make something so we can get him out of here?"

Ignatius ran forward.

Then surprising everyone, Bruce slowly stood up.

Was it some sort of miracle, or part of the game? Perhaps fate was handing Bruce a second chance because of his heroic deed. Bruce lifted his hand in a wave, slowly moving it as if to tell everyone to keep moving and that he was alright. After two steps forward, Bruce stopped.

Ted swore he smiled, but it was hard to tell.

The relief was short lived.

How he did it, no one would ever know. The pain had to be excruciating. Bruce turned and with what had to be every ounce and every bit of energy he had remaining, he charged back into the burning woods.

Everyone screamed out, 'No!' trying to stop him.

It didn't matter.

Bruce didn't make it far; his entire body was encompassed in flames in a few seconds. He dropped to his knees, then immediately after, fell forward. Sparking embers and flames shot upward when he landed.

There was no miracle, no second chance. It didn't matter what Bruce did, the lives he saved or how brave he was. Bruce was gone.

FIFTEEN

NAME SAKES

The Portal Five were now only four and they sat quietly, reeling in the aftermath of their friend's death.

They had retreated from Mingo Park and had driven thirty miles to get to a safe zone.

That was after they attempted to get home.

But there was no going home for Ted or Lincoln. Uncle Bob and Aunt Sally lived three blocks from Bea's house, and Lincoln's apartment was just on the edge of that borough. The entire area had been destroyed.

Fires ripped through the neighborhoods. Anywhere within a five-mile radius of Pittsburgh was off limits to vehicles.

Even though they wanted Officer Bill Smith to stay with them, he requested to be dropped off near his grandmother's neighborhood. He was swimming in regret for not going to get her. Despite the fact that it that it was dismal and her neighborhood was one of the ones feeling the effects of the dragon attack, he still had to look.

Just beyond the Pennsylvania border, they found an untouched area in West Virginia.

They stopped to take a breather, as had thousands of other people. The national guard along with FEMA had set up in parking lot of a Sporting Goods store right off the exit.

They were still deep in the danger zone, or on the game board as Uncle Bob called it.

School buses lined up by the dozens in the parking lot. All of them headed west, the shortest distance out of the circle. Some were headed to Louisville, some to Nashville and other various places.

The signup line was long for the buses, but there wasn't a wait to get the special packs that the Salvation Army was handing out. In each bag there were four bottles of water, a blanket, a toiletries kit and two MREs. Ted and Lincoln walked over with Uncle Bob to grab them.

Bea sat on the ground next to the van with Sally.

She wasn't her usual self: her face looked drawn and ten years older. She stood up when Ted and Lincoln returned.

"Did you get us on a bus?" she asked.

Ignatius approached and answered that question. "That isn't going to work. Bob knows it. Nashville, Louisville, all close to forest and mountains, safe havens for Dragons if they change direction. You need to go west. Preferably a desert or an area with very few forests."

149

"There are parts of Kansas," Bob said. "They may work. But how to get there is the question."

Ignatius pointed to a blue car that sat off to the side. "It's abandoned. It will run for you. It will get you to where you need to be. You need to go with your wife, Bob, and sister-in-law."

"I know. And you're sure the car is abandoned?"

"Pretty sure," Ignatius said. "I'll let you guys say goodbye. We'll be in the van."

"Goodbye?" Bea asked. "What did he mean? Are you not coming with us?" she asked Ted and Lincoln.

Lincoln shook his head. "No, we have to do this."

Bea nodded. "I understand. It breaks my heart, I'll worry. Oh, boy will I worry, but I know this is what you need to do."

"It sounds strange saying it," Lincoln said. "But we started it. We have to finish."

Bea peered around Lincoln to the others. "I'm so sorry about your friend. I can't believe what he did for us."

"Yeah," Ted said. "That was pretty awesome. I'll never forget it. But ... we have to go."

Lincoln embraced his mother, then Aunt and finally Bob. "We'll be back, I promise."

"We're gonna end this mom." Ted hugged his mother. "We are. I don't know how, I don't know when or where, but we will." His eyes cast downward in sadness. "I wish ... I wish we had those super abilities. Something to rely on. We don't but we're gonna do the best we can."

"Remember," Uncle Bob said. "Sometimes it doesn't take strength, sometimes all it takes is heart. You two could run away from this, but you're not. That says a lot. Now go. You got this."

As they stepped away, a woman's voice rang out in the sky. It was deep, sultry and sexy as she said. "Rank achieved … bravery rewarded."

"Aw," Bea said out proudly. "That's so nice, who said that? See boys, I told you that you did so good trying to help Bruce."

Ted faced Lincoln. "Rank achieved?"

"Bravery rewarded?" Lincoln asked. "What the heck does that mean?"

It was time to go.

<><><><>

Ninety-two minutes. That was how long they drove in silence until Ignatius slapped his hand on the table and said, "Enough."

"What is enough?" Basa asked.

"This. This quiet moping stuff. Enough," Ignatius said.

"Dude, your friend, our new friend, just died," said Ted.

"He not only died. He died saving our mother and aunt," Lincoln added.

"Not meaning to make it sound like a joke," Ted said. "But he went out in a blaze of glory."

"How is that a joke?" Ignatius said. "He literally went out in a blaze of glory. And Bruce would not want us to be this way."

"I'm pretty sure," Lincoln said., "He would be okay with a little mourning three hours after his death."

"Nope." Ignatius shook his head. "I'm pretty sure he wouldn't be. I'm also pretty sure that we are being like this because he didn't die killing a dragon. Which is how members of our team usually go out."

"He knew," Samuelson said. "He knew. Maybe not consciously, but inside he knew. He gave that pep talk to Ted. Barbarians always get smart before they expire."

Paxton chuckled a little. "Do you remember what Bruce was like when the Lioness died when the draco bit off her head?"

Basa laughed. "He said he never liked her."

"And," Paxton said. "Did he mourn in silence when the Jumper thought he could jump and catch the draco. No. They were friends. They indulged in drink nightly and laughs. But Bruce, he drank his ale then tossed it over the cliff for his friend and went on the next day. You are right, Ignatius he wouldn't want us like this."

"No." Ignatius shook his head. "And I remember when the Butcher was roasted by the dragon, what did Bruce do? He sliced a piece of dragon, cooked and ate it."

"He ate dragon?" Ted asked.

"He did. We all did," Ignatius said.

"How … how does it taste?"

"It needed seasoning but otherwise much like pigeon," Ignatius replied.

Paxton scoffed. "More like rabbit."

"Rabbit?" Ignatius laughed. "It was super tender."

"It tasted a bit wild," said Basa. "I didn't care for it."

"The point is being made ..." Samuelson said, "None of us are behaving like Bruce would behave. We must honor his memory and sacrifice by smiling at his memory and doing what he would do."

Silence.

"Um ..." Ted stammered. "I don't think anyone can do what he did."

"Then we do what we can to make up for it," Samuelson said. "We all have a special skill set."

Lincoln laughed. "I'm pretty sure me and my brother do not have a special skill set. We can't know all, or manifest, yield a wicked flaming sword or enchant people."

"Maybe not," Samuelson replied. "But you have something. You wouldn't still be with our quest team if you didn't. You battled with us and won."

"As much as we want cool superpowers," Ted said. "We don't have them or won't."

"First of all," Ignatius said. "They aren't called superpowers. They're as Samuelson said, skills. Through your impressive deeds you gain new skills or ranks in existing skills, especially after winning a dragon battle. Uncle Bob was named the Warrior, he became more powerful."

"And ..." Lincoln said. "There was silence and nothing for us."

153

"Dude." Ted reached over and backhanded Lincoln's arm. "The chick voice that came out of nowhere. Rank achieved. Bravery rewarded. That has to be what it means."

"But what were our rewards?" Lincoln shifted his eyes to Ignatius. "Has that happened before? A woman calling out bravery rewarded?"

"Yes, several times. Usually before a big battle when someone new joins us," Ignatius said. "When she says 'Rank achieved' it means the player has become a hero, but your roles haven't been determined. Butcher was Butcher after slaying the dragon. Jumper was made the jumper right before the battle."

Basa laughed. "He was so not happy about that."

"No, he wasn't," said Ignatius. "But as he learned. All skills earned are valuable at some point."

"It's a little different," Lincoln said. "You guys aren't from around here. It may not work that way in our world."

"Plus," Ted added. "You're the Portal Five."

"No, we're not," Ignatius said.

"Sorry," Ted replied, sadly. "It's habit. Portal Four."

"No." Ignatius shook his head. "Like it or not, you're part of this quest. So, actually, we're the Portal Six."

<><><><><>

It was strange, almost super strange to Ted. When they arrived at area near Butler Knob a military blockade was set up, much like

154

the one in Farmington. When they pulled up, the soldier that approached the van looked relieved.

"Please tell me you guys are the Slayer, Wizard, Prince, Barbarian and Fairy."

Ted didn't feel like getting into specifics about the fate of Bruce, he just leaned over Lincoln toward the driver's window and said, "We are."

The troops removed the barricade and let them right in, instructing them to park off to the side and go to where a large tent had been set up.

They disembarked and as they walked to the tent, everyone they passed waved and nodded hello. Ted expected to see Colonel Hansen when they stepped inside the tent. Instead, they were greeted by an older woman who stood with a man in a military uniform, looking over a table.

"Our dragon slayers," the woman said with an extended hand. "I'm Secretary of Defense Macy Lawrence, you can call me Macy, that's fine. And this ..." She pointed to the man. "Is General Hallsworth. So glad to meet you gentlemen... and lady. We have heard so much about you."

"Thanks," Ted said.

"Let me see um ... wings." She pointed to Ignatius. "You're the Fairy. And you ... you look like Sam Elliott. Hansen told me about you. You're the Wizard. Princess?" She pointed to Basa.

"Slayer. He is the Prince." Basa shook her head and indicated to Paxton.

"Madam." Paxton bowed. "It is an honor to meet you."

"Aren't you enchanting," she said.

"More than you know."

"And the Barbarian?" she asked.

"He …" Ted began to explain. "Is …"

Suddenly, a deep male voice echoed from above the tent. "Bravery reward. Barbarian restored."

Everyone looked up.

An even deeper voice came from Lincoln. "It is I. Barbarian."

"Dude?" Ted asked. "What was that?"

"I …" Lincoln cleared his throat. "I don't know."

"The gods have spoken," Ignatius pointed to Lincoln. "He may not look it, but he is a Barbarian."

"Wow, wonderful, and you?" she asked Ted.

"Bravery rewarded…" the mystery male voice spoke. "Thinker created."

"Thinker?" Ted looked up. "I'm the Thinker?"

Ignatius nudged him. "Beggars can't be choosers."

Macy seemed oblivious to the side conversation as she clapped her hands together once and announced, "Now that we all have met, join us at the table. We'll go over things."

Ted reached out to Ignatius holding him back as the others passed. "Thinker? The Thinker?" he asked in a whisper. "What does that even mean? I've never played a game with a Thinker class."

"You'll find out, I guess. It's your special skill."

"But my brother is the Barbarian reincarnate?"

Ignatius shrugged. "Once you are given your class, you obtain relevant special skills. That's the way it works. Obviously, something in you spurned the might of the Barbarian or the gods would have given you that."

"I'm as strong as he is, so why is Link the Barbarian? I should have been the Barbarian." Ted walked to the table to join the others.

It had to be the biggest iPad-looking tablet Ted had ever seen. Set on the table, the large rectangle of glass displayed a 3D map with some yellow lights and three deep purple lights.

Ted didn't need to be an expert on what they were.

"This is where they returned to this morning," Macy said. "Same location when they first arrived, but different dragons. These right here." She pointed to the purple lights. "Are dragons."

"There's only three," said Ignatius. "I thought you said there are four"

"There are," the general said. "One has been in the sky constantly as a look out. They have alternated twice. We tried to shoot them down, they got us. We sent in heat seeking missiles ... they ate them."

"Which is why we need you," Macy said. "It's like they have some radar or know exactly what we're doing. But that wasn't the case with you guys down by Farmington. Somehow, you were able to take them down with ease."

Samuelson nodded. "We have been doing it for some time."

"And," Basa added. "You must know, you are attempting the slaughtering during the day. They see very well in the daylight."

Lincoln added. "But that wouldn't make a difference with the missiles, I'm betting they sense them."

"Chances of success increase," said Paxton. "If you take them at night. We shall form a group and head to the mountain top this evening."

"And we'll give you any assistance you need," Macy told them, then pointed to the map. "This road leads to the top. It's one point five miles long. We are going to set up camp, third ridge down. Other than walking through the woods, which to me sounds dangerous, this road is a clear access to them. And they know it. This is where they seem to have set up some sort of line of defense." She pointed to the yellow lights. We can't figure out what they are. Do you have any idea what they are, Mr. Fairy?"

"Bunnies," Ignatius said. "They have to be the bunnies. A line of defense for them like in Farmington."

The general stifled a laugh. "Bunnies."

"Oh, dude," Ted said. "They aren't your normal Peter Cotton Tail." He lifted his leg to the table, raised his pant leg and removed the bandage.

Macy's eyes widened. "The … bunnies did that?"

"Yep." Ted nodded and lowered his leg. "And you can't see them the dark. But what if …." He looked at the map. "What is the distance between this ridge and the top?"

"Third of a mile," Macy answered.

"Do we know what they're doing up there?" Ted asked.

"We can only see them moving with radar," Macy replied. "Any attempt at getting an aerial view, even with a drone has been thwarted."

"Eyes on the sky," Ted said. "They're watching the sky." He raced the others. "If they're expecting us, they won't expect us until night fall. Ignatius, you guys have been super predictable."

"Excuse me," the general interrupted. "But you're making it sound like these things are intelligent."

"They are," Ted replied. "They have this higher intelligence we can't understand. So … can we … go now and eliminate the first line of defense they have."

"Take out the bunnies?" Ignatius asked.

"Take them out, that way we can safely go after them in the dark," Ted said. "They will have no first line of defense."

"There's another obstacle," the general said. "Where they are now used to be a building and communication tower. They destroyed that and about twenty feet before the …" he cleared his throat. "Bunnies, they dropped that tower and some rubble. Climbing over it would take some time. Going around it isn't as possible because at that exact point they dropped it, the sides of the road drop down about forty feet on both sides."

Ignatius ran his hand across his chin. "So, they were very strategic about where they placed it."

"Very," the general replied. "Like a mini obstacle course."

"But this shouldn't be a problem," Macy said brightly. "I mean, a small area would need to be cleared to get through."

The general shook his head. "Too risky, that would involve bringing trucks up there and that would be too much noise."

"That's not what I'm talking about," Macy said. "Mr. Barbarian." She faced Lincoln. "You have exhibited great feats of strength, I am sure this isn't an issue."

Lincoln's mouth formed a circle as he stammered to find the right words.

Ignatius spoke up. "Nah, you're right. He can do it."

"Dude!" Lincoln faced him. "Really?'

"You're good, big guy," Ignatius slapped him on the back.

Lincoln mouthed the words, 'big guy?' with a question.

"We can do this," Paxton said. "We will use our bow and arrows to eliminate the bunnies. In the daylight they will be fair game."

Ted snickered. "Fair game. Game. Bunnies are game." No response. "Never mind."

"Wait. No. Stop," Lincoln said. "It's daylight. The dragons can still see us. If they hear us, we don't have the advantage of the dark."

"What if we send up an elite force with you," the general suggested. "With firing power. We know one of you shot one down with standard weapons."

"Check this out," Lincoln said. "Not sure if you know this. They breathe fire. They spit fire like a freaking blow torch. They'll torch us as soon as they see us, before the elite team can fire."

Samuelson looked down to the electronic map. "The red areas are the draconem, correct? You can see them moving."

Macy nodded. "And we can monitor the one flying."

"Can you communicate some way with us?" Samuelson asked. "Let us know they are coming. Telepathy perhaps, or by carrier pigeon?"

"Will radios work?" asked Macy.

Ignatius answered. "Yes."

"Then this can work," Macy said. "Use the trees as cover on the way up until the barricade. We'll send a backup team with you and radio if the dragons move or the one circling can see you. What do you think, Ms. Slayer?"

"A daytime battle!" Basa chanted. "This will be wonderful."

Ignatius clapped his hands together once. "I'm excited." He turned to Lincoln. "Aren't you, big guy?"

Lincoln's only response was a low, throat grumble.

SIXTEEN

GIVE ME YOUR HAND

Sergeant Doug Mitchell was a self-proclaimed geek. Even though he was part of a bad-ass elite team called the Wolf Pack, armed like a bunch of Rambos, he started out his conversation with Ted by telling him, "Just so you know man, I'm a total geek."

Ted had no idea why Mitchell would announce this, nor why to Ted in particular. They had just left the base and started the journey up the mountain, walking off the road in the woods, not quite in the silent zone.

"So, Cap said, the rumor has it you think this is nothing more than a game. Like some fantasy world suddenly invaded earth."

Ted just looked at him, afraid to say anything.

"Look I'm not poking fun. It makes total sense if you think about it. I mean, it doesn't make sense but it does. Have you thought about whether we all now have character points and attributes?"

"That's interesting," Ted replied. "But if we have character sheets somewhere, I haven't found any way to view them."

Lincoln leaned over. "Just as well, bro', or you'd see your three in Charisma and Wisdom."

For a moment, Ted was speechless.

"Ha, win!" laughed Lincoln.

"We don't have time for this," muttered Ted, "right now we have to focus on taking out these dragons before they kill any more people."

"Bringing down the dragons just isn't gonna do it," said Doug, "if it's a game, it's not going to end by winning battles. You have to find the person creating the content."

"If ... and that's an if ..." Ted replied, "this is a game, then it's a hybrid shoot-em-up and RPG. But ... I'm not saying anything."

"I get it," Doug nodded. "But if you want to talk and get advice I'm here."

"I appreciate it."

"I had my own YouTube channel for a while. Pretty popular, Thirty thousand subscribers. I was shut down cause some idiot gamer said I reviewed his prototype when I didn't, terms of service and stuff and ..." Doug put his finger to his ear. "Roger that." He looked at Ted. "Okay, we go silent."

Ted wanted to say, 'Thank God', and that Doug really didn't need to repeat the order to Ted, as he had one of those earpieces as well. But Ted was polite, simply acknowledged the command, and hurried to catch up to his brother.

With only two years age difference, Ted and Lincoln had been best friends all of their lives. No other friend could compare to

Linc and it was even better that they were brothers. Years of staying up after bedtime and being quiet gave them the ability to communicate with just a glance and facial expressions.

Ted gave such a look to Lincoln: to ask if he was okay.

Lincoln replied by shaking his head.

A double pat to his brother's back was Ted's way of saying it would be fine.

Until they reached the point where they had to go back onto the road.

"So far all clear," Command said in the earpiece. "Bird in the sky is still at a distance and the three red riding hoods haven't moved."

Another voice came from the radio, it sounded like the captain. "Barbarian you're on."

A look of sheer panic came over Lincoln when the captain said that, and Ted saw his brother stare at the blocked area with total dismay.

The radio tower crossed the road. The top portion of which would be easy to climb over had it not been for the several pieces of a building that rested against it.

"Barbarian," the captain said. "If you can move that we can get through."

Ignatius walked up to Lincoln, whispering. "When you move them try not to make any noise. Set them down gently."

Lincoln's voice squeaked as he emotionally replied in a whisper. "Set them down gently? After I what? Lift them?"

"You can do it," Ignatius said.

"Look, I know I look strong," Lincoln said. "Maybe not, but if you would have seen me and Ted try to move my Aunt Sally's piano, you'd think twice about saying I can do this."

"Go."

"Fine," Lincoln spoke in a whispering grumble. "Everyone's counting on me. Biggest embarrassment of my life. You better have a backup story." He walked nervously to the first section of rubble. It looked like the dragons had played house of cards with concrete walls. He thought about the walls that Bruce had moved in Pittsburgh, how he crouched down like a weightlifter, gripping the wall. Lincoln resolved to give it a try, then he saw Paxton approach. "What?" he asked the Prince.

"You'll need my guidance to place it down."

"Sure." Lincoln crouched down, placing one hand behind the wall as he gripped the front. That was when he noticed Ted holding up the phone with a shitty look on his face.

He was videoing it? Lincoln was sure his brother would find a way to embarrass him with the recording when and if everything returned to normal.

Thinking, *here goes nothing but my back*, Lincoln tried to lift the concrete.

He expected it not to budge. He expected the only thing to move would be his hands up the wall and that disc in his back. But that wasn't the case.

He actually lifted the block and did so with ease. It didn't even feel like it weighed anything. With guidance from Paxton, he quietly set it off to the side.

He felt invincible and cool. No more strange looks at Arby's when the second freezer broke again and he would have to move it. It was on the third and final piece of rubble, with Lincoln enjoying the admiring looks from the rest of the team, that he had a realization: it wasn't him moving the stones. It was probably Ignatius, turning them weightless.

When he was finished and the captain gave the all clear, Lincoln walked up to Ignatius.

"Good job," Ignatius said.

"Well, I couldn't have done it without you. Thanks for not letting me look like a fool and giving me help there."

"Oh, I didn't help you at all," Ignatius said. "You did it. It's your strength."

"How?"

"You are now the Barbarian. It's the way it is. Not only have the gods rewarded you with ability, they bestowed the honor of carrying on the name for Barbarian. Just … just be prepared for a sudden urge to drink large amounts of ale, incredibly lude thoughts at inappropriate times and an overwhelming desire to find women with three breasts."

Leaving behind a speechless Lincoln who thought he was joking, Ignatius joined the others in crossing over the downed power tower.

<>< >< >< >

Excitedly, and still speaking in a whisper, Lincoln walked up to his brother. "Dude, did you see that?"

"Dude, I did." Ted lifted his phone. "I got it all on camera."

"Sweet."

"Now that you opened the way, let's go get them bunnies," Ted said, "I am curious what they look like in the day."

"They were ugly at night."

"My leg still hurts."

Ignatius was the first through the new opening, he waved impatiently for Ted and Lincoln to catch up, and they did.

The Wolf Pack elite force held up the rear.

The road bent slightly after the blockade and short jaunt up a small hillside brought the area into view where they bunnies were supposed to be.

Only they weren't bunnies.

The immobility of the creatures ruled that out.

There were dozens of them perched about the thick grassy area.

Soon the soldier had joined them on that grassy ridge.

"What are they?" Ted asked.

Samuelson bent down to one. He looked over his shoulder at everyone else. "Dragon eggs."

Ted moved near Samuelson and crouched down to get a better look. There was something scary and beautiful about them at the same time.

The slope was covered with oval objects the size of a football, which would have been almost completely translucent if it weren't for the hard substance that bound the eggs like a vine.

The outer layer didn't stop Ted from seeing what was inside the nearest one. Surrounded by a golden fluid, a dragon fetus looked like a lizard; the wings hadn't formed.

"It's early enough to slaughter them," said Samuelson. "The question is how. Once we touch one, the dragons will come."

"That's a good thing," Ted said. "If they come, they're protecting them. If they're protecting them, they won't light this place up."

"Good thinking."

"Well," Ignatius said. "He is the Thinker."

Basa turned around. "We pierce the shell and release the fluid. It would be a silent way to do so and the contents will die. There are twelve of us. We each only have to do three each. We coordinate and do it quickly."

Ted stood. "See I'm thinking differently."

Ignatius tossed out his hands. "Give him a little ability and he just can't stop."

"No, hear me out," Ted explained. "We destroy these eggs, those dragons are gonna be full of vengeance. Right now, they're staying close to protect these. These are still too new to hatch, first we should take out the dragons, then we can worry about these."

"Which leads me to wonder," Lincoln said. "If these aren't the line of defense, what is?"

They heard an, "Oh, no," from Paxton.

Lincoln looked. "What the hell?"

"This isn't good," Ignatius said.

Finally, Ted looked. If he wasn't seeing it with his own eyes he would not have believed it. It stood in the middle of the field of dragon eggs.

Doug stepped to the group. "Is that …"

"Yes," Samuelson answered. "A unicorn."

It wasn't big like a horse, in fact, to Ted it was a textbook example of a *My Little Pony* unicorn. Its body was white, little and a bit stubby. Its mane and tail were flowing streams of purple and pink. It had big giant eyelashes and the alicorn on top of its head looked like strawberry and vanilla swirl soft serve ice cream.

"Ah," Ted softly gushed. "Look how cute."

Basa turned to Ted. "Do not let the appearance deceive you my friend. They are vicious."

"What?" Ted nearly laughed. "No way."

"Yes," Ignatius replied. "Trust me they don't puke rainbows and shit glitter."

"We must slay it," said Basa. "Take it down quickly before it charges"

"No way. And kill it?" Ted asked. "Seems a harsh. It's so innocent looking."

"Get it together," Ignatius snapped. "We need a plan."

Doug said. "We can shoot it."

Ignatius shook his head. "No, it will call the dragons."

"I know," said Paxton. "I will enchant it. While it is mesmerized by my charm, Basalous can behead it."

Ted cringed.

"Good plan," Ignatius told him them turned to Doug. "Have your best shooters ready in case this goes south."

"Have faith," Paxton told him. "We will handle this. Basalous, stay close, but wait until you see it is under my spell."

Ted didn't want to watch. It seemed so cruel and the little unicorn appeared so harmless. It stood in the field, sniffing the dragon eggs, its tail swinging happily.

Paxton approached it and the unicorn noticed him.

As Paxton drew closer, the unicorn made a chirping, gerbil type sound, swinging its head so happily.

"There, there," Paxton said softly. "My new little friend." He inched closer, one hand behind his back gripping a sword, while he held the other out as if to show he meant no harm, "You are so beautiful. Yes, you are."

At a foot away, the unicorn stopped swinging its tail and swaying its head. It stared frozen at Paxton.

Basa crept up quickly, firing up the swords.

"That's right, you love me," Paxton said.

Just as Basa approached, the sweet innocent look on the unicorn's face turned wicked. Its little mouth no longer looked puckered and ready to kiss, but rather ready to bite. It opened its mouth exposing large, sharp hyena teeth and with a quick snap of its jaws took off Paxton's arm right below the elbow.

He couldn't make a noise, and Paxton buckled, his mouth wide as he released a silent scream while blood shot from his arm.

The shock of the unicorn attack on Paxton startled Basa and she stumbled back, the swipe of a sword only taking off the animal's tail.

Jumping to its hind legs, the unicorn jerked his head, spat out Paxton's arm and charged the rest of the group.

Basa tried to strike it again, but only tore a gash in the beast's flank.

"Man down, man down," Doug called out. "Medic." He raised his weapon and fired three shots, striking the unicorn in its run.

The tailless animal, bleeding from the neck and side of the head, dropped to the ground with weakened legs. It landed on its side, then quickly scrambled up again. Before it could revive enough to charge again, Basa succeeded in a final blow. Beheading the animal with a slice to the base of its neck.

The head of the unicorn popped off and rolled, its colorful mane covered its face when it came to a stop.

A godly voice speaking out of nowhere in the pandemonium was barely noticed by anyone but Ignatius.

"The … Sharpshooter. Rank achieved."

Ignatius looked then to Doug before looking back to the Prince.

A solder had run to Paxton, trying to give aid and was already at his side, when Lincoln and Ted ran to him as well.

"What's going on up there?" Macy's voice came through the radio. "Get out. Get out now. The dragons: all four are coming."

Being the new Barbarian, it was Lincoln who had to sweep Paxton into his arms, and run with him, the medic running alongside, keeping pressure on the amputated limb.

Everyone fled that area, running down the small grade, through the barricade and down the road until they veered off into the trees.

"Down," Ignatius said. "Stay close to the ground. Cover with foliage. No noise."

Ted slid down next to his brother. Lincoln and the medic bodily covered Paxton, and Ted hurriedly threw as many leaves as he could over them. He inched down finding a place under a fallen tree and listened as the dragons roared and screeched.

It seemed like an hour passed with the dragons flying overhead, crying out in what sounded like anger and determination.

Finally, the screeching faded.

"They returned," Macy said in the earpiece. "The one flew off. Come now. Fast."

They didn't need to be told twice, everyone jumped up.

For their own safety and Paxton's life, they had to get off that hill and to base as quick as possible.

Their day had been long. It was hard to believe it was barely four in the afternoon and already they had failed in their first simple mission up the mountain, and nearly lost Paxton in the process. After making it back to base, Paxton was rushed into a medic tent, while the others waited in the war room.

They sat in sad silence, no one speaking.

"Okay, I have news," Macy said as she entered.

Everyone stood up.

"They stabilized the Prince. He looks good. Right now Paxton is on his way to a combat support hospital in Fort Campbell where they are really good with amputations. Outlook is good, guys."

Everyone sighed out in relief.

"In fact," Macy continued. "He was conscious and talking. His spirits are good. They sedated him for the trip, but … as you know, he will not be able to fight with you. He's out for a while."

"Then we will take him," Ignatius pointed to Doug. "He is the Sharpshooter."

"I'm not that good," said Doug.

"You will be now," Ignatius replied.

"Good. Good," Macy said. "You need a team. I'll make him an official member of your special squad. And you'll need more. You'll need all the help you can get. Radar just picked up three more dragons that appeared out of nowhere over Erie and are headed this way."

"What!" Ignatius blasted. "Three more?"

Macy nodded. "Three more. Now, I'll leave you people be. To think. Plan. Sergeant Mitchell," she spoke to Doug. "Come with me to speak to the general."

"Yes, Ma'am," he replied and followed her out.

"Seven," Ignatius said in defeat as he sat back down.

Basa paced. "They are on their way here. It is daylight, they are not attacking. Why?"

"Maniacal Master must be planning a larger strike," said Samuelson. "We do know, we get reprieves. Once and a while, it stops, but then continues."

"A day or two break," Basa said. "Perhaps this is our chance to gain advantage."

"We don't know that," Samuelson replied. "For all we know tomorrow at dawn, the force of seven could annihilate us all."

"Seven," Ignatius huffed. "What is going on? Seven. Never have there been seven."

"But there is now," Ted stated. "So get over it and start planning for that."

"Two was tough. Three was doable," Ignatius said. "How are we supposed to slaughter seven? Not three, not two, but seven."

"Why?" Ted asked, "are you so stuck on this pattern. Things change."

"But he never has. He all but told us this is his routine," Ignatius said.

"Huh?" Lincoln asked. "I thought none of you actually met him. Only some blue guy in the sky. How did he tell you it's his routine?"

"Because it's in his name," Ignatius answered.

"His name?" Ted asked.

"Yes. Maniacal Master Three, Two, Three."

Ted froze in a stare.

"Ted?" Lincoln snapped his finger in front of Ted's face.

"Oh. My. God." Ted turned, placing his back to everyone as he walked across the tent. "Oh my God."

"What? What?" Lincoln asked with impatience.

Ted spun around and smacked himself on the forehead. "It's his name! Maniacal Master three-two-three. We can get him." He moved to Ignatius. "You manifest things. Can you, I know this is outlandish, but can you manifest a time machine?"

"Ted," Lincoln chuckled his name. "Please, stop. Don't be ridiculous."

"I'm not being ridiculous. Can you?" he asked Ignatius.

"No, but ..." he pointed to Samuelson. "He can."

"I can, however..." Samuelson answered, "you can do little more than observe or you will be cast into the void. You can not go back and create any contradiction with this timeline. You can not go back and stop yourself from opening the portal."

"Oh, I'm not going to," Ted said. "If we didn't open it, someone else would have. No, I need to go back to use the internet, to go online before all this started."

175

"Why?" Ignatius asked.

"You gave me his name," Ted said. "I think I can find him. Two days before. That's all I need. Two days before."

Lincoln asked. "Why two days? Why not the day before or week."

"Because I know where I was," Ted replied. "The store was slow, they sent me home and I went to the Gregory Peck Fest at the Hollywood."

"Oh, Dude," Lincoln shook his head. "Really. Gregory Peck?"

"Doesn't matter. It was great by the way," Ted stated. "Sam, can you do it?"

Samuelson sighed out heavily, almost annoyed. "It's my least favorite ability. But yes, I can do it. However, I need something from the time frame and place you want to go. That's not so easy."

Ted reached into his back pocket, pulled out a ticket stub. "Will this work."

Samuelson took it and looked down at it. "Yes, it will." He looked around the tent, then after what seemed like a failed attempt at finding something, he stepped outside. He returned with a small rock. "Place this in your pocket. This is from right now, right here." He handed it to Ted.

"Okay." Ted placed it in his front pocket.

"Do not lose it. When you are ready to return, drop it to the ground and step on it," Samuelson instructed. "It will bring you right back to the exact same spot, same time, a split second after you leave."

"Got it."

"If you must speak to someone you know, say nothing that can change anything."

Ted nodded.

"Be quick. Do what needs to be done and get right back," Samuelson instructed.

"I need an hour, two tops."

"You're really time traveling?" Lincoln asked. "Have you thought this through?"

"I don't need to think it through," Ted replied. "I know what has to be done."

"Is he really time traveling?" Lincoln asked Samuelson.

"He is," Samuelson replied.

"Shit. You're lucky. Is it safe?" questioned Lincoln.

"No, it is extremely dangerous. Should he tread on the wrong butterfly we will never see him again. He must follow the rules and get right back."

"I will," Ted said with confidence. "And I've never trodden on any butterflies."

Ignatius stepped to him, placing his hands on Ted's arms. "You truly think you can find the Master?"

"Oh, for sure, I really do," Ted replied.

"I am proud," Ignatius said. "Perhaps The Thinker truly was the name for you."

"Let's hope." Ted looked at Samuelson. "How long do you need to get ready do this."

"Please, I am a Wizard. I am all-knowing, all-powerful. I'll do this now." He lifted the ticket stub. "I will use this to create the door. When you step through you will arrive right where this is from."

"Perfect." Ted took a deep breath. "Let's do this."

Lincoln stepped to Ted and embraced him. "Good luck."

"Thanks." Ted replied and nodded to Samuelson. "Ready."

Samuels, holding the ticket stub between his forefinger and thumb, moved his arm in a circular motion. He moved it around and around until a bright vivid light appeared, surrounding what looked like a mini portal. "Be well. Be safe. Good fortune."

Ted stepped toward the hole.

"My friend, the Thinker, may you find …" Basa said. "All that …"

Ted stepped through. The portal closed.

Basa's arm dropped as the words trailed off. "You need and good …"

Another bright light appeared suddenly and out of thin air, Ted stepped back through.

"Fortune," Basa finished her sentence then looked confused. "Did it not work?"

Ted looked at everyone then lifted a manila folder. "Oh, it worked, alright" He grinned widely. "I got it."

SEVENTEEN

FINDING NEEMO

The folder, thick with papers, dropped to the table without losing a single sheet.

Ted stood proudly.

Lincoln lifted the folder. "You … got all this? How long were you there?"

"Four hours, only because the librarian was having preschool reading hour and I had to wait for her to get me the papers from the printer," Ted replied.

"You went to the library?" Lincoln asked.

"Oh, yeah. When I stepped through, man was it weird," Ted explained. "I walked through right smack in front of the theater. I knew I couldn't go home to use the computer, so I went to the library."

Ted stepped through the library doors and couldn't remember when he was there last. It looked different, they probably remodeled. He approached the desk. "Excuse me, can anyone use the computer and print up stuff?" he asked the woman behind the counter.

"Sure," she replied. "You need your library card number to log in."

"I don't have a library card."

"You don't have a library card?" she asked in disbelief. "I mean, it's okay if you don't have the physical card, I can look up the number."

"I don't think I ever bought one."

"You wouldn't have bought it, what is your full name?"

"Theodore Reagan Williams."

She glanced up at him, typed some and looked again. "Okay, yes, you have one."

"Cool."

"It's been suspended for sixteen years for overdue library fees," she said. "Just pay the fees and I'll get you a new card."

"How much."

"Seventy-three cents."

"Wait." Ted reached into his pocket. "You suspended my card for less than a buck?"

"I didn't do it, I was five back then."

He placed a dollar on the counter.

"And you got all this?" Lincoln asked.

"Yeah, it's a lot. It was like a map to the truth," Ted replied, the peered up when Macy walked in.

"I see a pow wow is happening," she said. "Have you come up with anything?"

"The Thinker…" Samuelson said, "has gone back in time and gained valuable information he is about to share."

"Back … in time?"

Lincoln said, "Don't ask. Just know he did it so he could get information off the internet."

"Question." said Macy. "If you needed to use the internet and a computer, why go back in time? We could have gotten you that."

"In case the Master deleted information after our world became a game under his control, but …" Ted said, "it turns out the game started long before we came in."

Macy nodded. "Some of the guys are saying this is some sort of supernatural event, I'm not gonna question or be cynical if this gives us a way out."

"It does," Ted stated. "Ignatius sparked the thought. He kept saying three dragons, then two, then, three. He told me the reason he thought this was a clue in the Maniacal Master's name. It's not that they are dumb, they don't have the technology we have. So when they hear Maniacal Master three-two-three, they think clue. We think …"

Lincoln exhaled as he said it. "User name."

"Bingo. Granted it was a whim that made me think this would work—"

"You are the Thinker," said Ignatius. "It will just come to you."

"It kinda did," said Ted. "But it was an intricate trail. At first, I put in Maniacal Master as one word and nothing came up. Absolutely nothing. But when I put it in as separate words, it was just too many results. So I added the words game and computer and …" Ted opened the folder. "He has a blog, that he started ten years ago. Called *Mind of the Maniacal Master*. Not many entries. Fifteen over an eight-month period. The last ones are him venting over his situation."

Basa looked at all the papers, "This internet must be a powerful tool."

"It is," Ted said.

"Okay, I'll ask," Lincoln said. "How do we know this is the same Maniacal Master in this situation?"

"At the point when I first found it, I didn't. The blog started out as a tip place for gamers. Maniacal Master is a self-proclaimed computer genius, avid RPG gamer and developer. Self-proclaimed."

"I'm sorry," Macy raised her hand. "RPG?"

"Role playing games," Ted explained. "Like *Dungeon and Dragons*. Anyhow, apparently this guy was accepted into three different high-end schools. He picked Carnegie Mellon and he dropped out because he said someone stole his game idea. One he called *Plight of the Draconem*. He was pissed, said he was gonna fight it. That everyone from Pittsburgh is a tech thief. He hates Pittsburgh, which makes sense that this area would be the one hit by dragons. I have a feeling it wouldn't matter who opened the game and clicked on the link, Pittsburgh would still be hit."

"So …" Ignatius said. "If someone stole his game, then someone else is pretending to be him."

Ted waved a finger. "I had that brief thought. Until I read this…" he shuffled to a paper and lifted it, reading, "*People have always been jealous of me, never treated me with respect. I'm different. I tried to share my RPG game idea on the* Games, Dames, and Dragons *forum, but they banned me because I told them my father was a fairy. Which is true, but they never let me explain that, and they claimed I was a bigot and kicked me off.*"

Lincoln looked at Ignatius. "Is that possible? Can his father be a fairy?"

"You mean can a fairy father a child to a human woman?" Ignatius shrugged. "I suppose if the fairy is into that sort of thing. Most fairies are not attracted to humans. I mean, it would be like you being attracted to a goat."

"Dude." Lincoln cringed. "Not even close to the same thing."

"You don't think?"

"Anyhow!" Ted interrupted. "I decided to search the *Games, Dames and Dragons* forum thinking the post would not be deleted, but it was worth a shot." He handed Lincoln. "From fourteen years ago. Look at the user name."

Lincoln glanced down. "MM three-two-three. So … this guy isn't young."

"He's not old. Look at the reaction he got to the 'my dad is a fairy' thing."

Lincoln read, "*Not cool. You shouldn't say that about your dad. You should respect what he is and accept him.*" Lincoln peered up.

"That's funny. He's being serious about being part fairy and these guys think he's bashing his dad."

Macy shook her head. "How is this helping us?"

"Wait," Ted said. "Gotta let you know how it unfolds, if I don't tell you how I got there, you'll ask how I know. Link, you only read the reactions. Just read the first line of his post."

Lincoln did. "*I created an RPG game when I was twelve years old and would like to share it as an RPG here. The game is called ...*" Lincoln looked up. "*Dragons of Aberly.*"

The reading of that game name caused everyone to vocally react with questions.

"Twelve years old," Ted said. "Twelve. This guy has built this world since he was twelve. And he took it the site RPG Dungeons and started playing it there." Ted pointed to the folder. "Everything that's happened, happen in that RPG fourteen years ago. All these people playing helped create the story. But I saw it all, the whole thing."

Lincoln grabbed the folder and started to flip through. "Jesus," he said in shock. "He has all the names. Wizard, Paxton the Prince, Bruce the Barbarian, Ignatius the Fairy, Sam the Wizard."

"For real?" Macy hovered over Lincoln's shoulder and the others gathered in.

"Ted," Lincoln said. "This game goes on forever."

"Yeah, it does. I mean there were more, like the Butcher and stuff. The players were cutthroat," Ted replied. "So good that the Maniacal Master decided he wanted to take the game to a different level. He wrote a series of short stories, based on the game and posted them online. On the same site under fan fiction forum. People loved them."

"It was gamer fiction," Lincoln said. "Before gamer fiction."

Ted nodded. "Exactly. The fan feedback was intense and Maniacal really upped the anti of the stories. He threw in buffs and debuffs. Like Barbarian was supposed to be resistant to fire. And then he wasn't, so he died. Maniacal gave a buff to the unicorn to make him immune to the effects of the Prince. And that was how the Prince died in the story. Soon after, Basa dies by the mob of goblins."

Basa drew up a look of disgust. "Goblins?" She shivered. "Nasty creatures, they save your teeth. And a mob of them?"

"Yeah." Ted nodded. 'That happens and the dragon eggs are sprinkled by some witch named Louhi."

Again, Basa shuttered. "I hate her."

"Well you'll hate her even more," Ted said. "The eggs hatch and Wizard is eaten by all the baby dragons."

"Good Goddess on a mountain!" Wizard exclaimed.

"The stories end. That was the finale. The world is enveloped by dragons who protect the Master's lair and he only spares people who bring him things. Ignatius is the only one who doesn't die, he is banished to the dark dungeon for all eternity."

Samuelson exhaled. "A fate we all fear."

"I think he spared Ignatius," Ted said. "Because of his adulation for fairies."

"Wait. Ted, hold on," Lincoln said. "The last post on the forum was two years ago. How is this a game now? I mean you had RPG but then stories."

"It's a game being played. He is playing it. Master Maniacal was a self-proclaimed computer genius. Right? I am thinking he developed the computer version of the RPG and story. Made it his own game. I found him on social, media. Look where he says he works."

Lincoln read it, "Dungeon Gaze Inc,"

"The creators and website for *Wind and War*. So I went on the site, right. He's not listed as a developer, he's listed as a programmer, but … are you ready for this. Dungeon Gaze Inc is having an in-house contest for the next big game. The developer who wins get a hundred grand and lifetime supply of energy drinks and Doritos."

"Dude, he's trying to win the contest," Lincoln said.

"But he has to test the game. So …I think he hacked the end of *Wind and War*, created some sort of funnel that takes you to his game, this game we're in right now."

"Where he sat," Lincoln said. "Waiting for someone to click play."

"We were the first. He's playtesting the game right now," Ted replied.

Macy raised both her hands. "This all sounds fantastical, but none of it explains how he had the power to make this all real."

"The very beginning explains it all," Ted said. "Ignatius, what is the Fairy's ability?"

"To Manifest," Ignatius replied and seeing that Macy looked confused, added, "to bring into reality objects by thinking about them."

"Including a game?" Macy asked.

"Yep," Ted said. "Let's assume fairies are real. And if MM really is part fairy, then he has the ability to manifest."

"He lived and breathed the game and stories all those years," Macy said. "It manifested into a reality."

"The moment we clicked 'enter'," Ted stated.

Ignatius pointed to the folder. "We have it all here. Everything that is going to happen. How do we stop it?"

"We don't," Ted replied. "We stop him. The man, the player. All one in the same. Because he's playing somewhere in his mom's basement. I won't judge that though, he's probably paying her bills."

"But we don't know who he is," Macy said.

"Yeah we do. I found him on social media. Remember me telling you about his game being stolen. I did a court case search using his game name and found him. He tried to sue and lost." Ted smiled triumphantly. "His name is Harold Neemo. He lives at three-two-three Pine Street, La Motte …" He gave a smile to Lincoln. "Iowa."

"Oh my God, it is some kid playing a video game in Iowa." Lincoln gushed.

"Probably a man, but we can stop him."

"Yes." Macy drew her fist in with excitement. "I'll get authorities out there right now. We'll shut his shit down."

"That won't end the problem of the world being a game," Ted told her.

"Why not?"

Lincoln explained. "He controls the game and the dragons. We simply shut him down, the dragons aren't controlled, they'll go rogue, and they'll be harder to stop."

"So what do we do?" she asked.

Ted answered. "We talk to him. We get him to finish the game, to put in some game-ending quest that restores our world."

"Who goes?" Macy asked. "Do I send the sheriff?"

"No," Lincoln answered. "The best ones to go are Ted … he figured this all out and … Ignatius because, well, Harold is a fairy so … he may believe Ignatius easier."

Macy nodded a few seconds taking it in. "Then it's a plan. Get ready Ted, I'll have you and Mr. Fairy on a plane in a half an hour. The rest of you stay back, stand by and work with my men in case this doesn't work. I'll get on that plane." She thanked Ted and walked out.

"Wonderful job," Samuelson told Ted.

"I agree," Ignatius said. "I am super impressed."

"I have faith in you," Basa said. "That I shall not have to meet my fate at the hands of a mob of goblins."

"Thank you," Ted replied almost bashfully.

"Bro." Lincoln placed his hand on Ted's back. "That was really good. You did kick ass research. I'm proud."

"Thanks."

"You do know you could have like skipped everything and just said the guy's name is Harold Neemo from Iowa and we have to stop him."

"Yeah, I know," Ted said. "But if we're playing a game, might as well have all the theatrics of it."

Ted gathered up the folder and all the papers that made their way out. He would bring it with him on the plane, read it all again. He wanted to make sure he knew everything.

They were headed into the end game, and Ted was determined they wouldn't lose.

EIGHTEEN

REASON

It was a long day and it was going to be an even longer night. Lincoln sipped a cup of coffee inside the war room tent. He worried and was anxious about his brother but felt a little at ease when they received word that his mother, aunt and Bob were settled in a camp for the night outside of Fort Campbell. He wanted them to go further west, but if all went well, there would be no need.

Yet, he was concerned how it would all play out.

In order for the Maniacal Master to end the game, he would have to create a quest line for them to complete, which meant they still might have to face the dragons and whatever else the Maniacal Master previously programmed and had planned for them.

They were exhausted and now there really only was himself, Basa and the new Sharpshooter guy. Sure, they had soldiers ready to go, but they, like Lincoln, lacked experience in fighting dragons.

"Good news," Macy said as she entered the tent. "They landed about twenty minutes ago and should be on their way to Harold Nemo's home."

"That's great to hear." Lincoln stood.

"Do you have any guesses what's next?" she asked. "The general and I need to know the plan."

"I am almost as new to this as you are," Lincoln said. "I keep thinking we will still have to fight the dragons. It might be easier, but it will still be tough."

Basa walked over to the pair. "Show me to your warriors. I will guide them and advise them of defeating dragons."

"That may not be a bad idea," Macy replied.

"Excuse me, Ma'am," a soldier walked in the tent. "I hate to interrupt but we have a very strange situation on our hands."

"What is it?" she asked.

"There appears to be a large group of … little people with crazy hair coming down the hill toward base."

"Little people?" she asked, then turned her head when Basa gasped loudly. "What is it Slayer?"

"Large group. A mob" Basa said. "They are goblins."

<><><><>

The house was a small frame house with a nice detached garage. Located on a flat street with a dozen other houses, the home had a maintained lawn and giant snail lawn ornaments.

191

Ted and Ignatius stood on the welcome mat before the front door.

Ignatius grabbed Ted's hand, stopping him from ringing the bell. "I have to ask you something."

"What is it?"

"If none of this is real, does that mean I'm not real and I'll vanish when the game is over?"

"I don't think so, I think either a portal will open up or you'll be here to stay. If you do stay, you're saving the world so I am pretty sure the government will make you a citizen."

"I don't want to disappear, Ted."

"You won't." Ted rang the bell. "Fairies must have existed before this all happened."

A few moments later, a woman answered the door. She looked very 'soccer mom'-like with short, full hair, a long, flowered tee shirt and tight yoga-style pants that clung to her curves.

"Hi," she said. "Can I … can I help you."

"Hi," Ted replied. "Are you Mrs. Neemo?"

"I am."

"We're looking for your husband, Harold," Ted said.

"Oh." She giggled and flung out her hand. "You mean my son. Are you friends of his?" she asked.

"You can say that," Ted replied. "We play one of his games with him. Does he live here?"

"He doesn't live here but he works from here. He can't get a strong enough signal at his apartment. He's been here for days.

Come on in." She held the door open wide, allowing them to pass inside. She looked at Ignatius. "You remind me of someone I knew years ago."

"You don't say," Ignatius replied.

"This way, he's downstairs." A short hall was directly in front of them. Mrs. Neemo walked down that hall, paused for a moment and looked into the living room. "I can't pull myself away from the news. It's horrible what's happening in Pennsylvania. All those people."

"It's pretty bad," Ted replied.

She continued down the hall and opened a door. "Harold!" she called.

No answer.

"Harold! Your friends are here."

Still no reply.

She shook her head. "Sometimes he wears those headphones and can't hear a darn thing. Go on down."

"Thank you, Ma'am," Ted said.

He and Ignatius walked past her and to the stairs. A few steps down, Ted jumped when the mother yelled down the steps again.

"Harold!'

"What is it Mom, I just started playing my game again. You know it has to be perfect."

"Your friends are coming down."

Ted and Ignatius arrived on the bottom step.

193

"Mom, what? You know I don't have any …" Harold turned around and set down the controller. "Who are you?"

<><><><>

"I shall lead the force," Basa drew her swords in the tent. "Gather your men, your marksmen, we shall take down the vile creatures before they know what hit them."

"We're just gonna gun them down?" Macy asked.

"If we don't. They will slice your legs, inhibit your ability to move, climb up your torso, snap open your jaw, reach down your throat, rip out your heart and steal your teeth."

"Oh my God." Macy exclaimed.

Swords raised, but not yet fiery, Basa raced from the tent, yelling out, "Charge."

"Charge?" Lincoln questioned then stepped out of the tent as well. He didn't hear any commotion so obviously the goblins weren't attacking yet.

Surely, someone would have screamed if their legs had been sliced and their heart ripped out.

Lincoln was curious as to what the goblins would look like. He envisioned a short person, with a slightly larger head, pointed nose and ears, with fierce teeth. They were probably hairy with burlap looking clothes. He wouldn't have even been surprised if they were some sort of version of a goblin from *Lord of the Rings*.

He didn't, in his wildest imagination, expect them to look like they did. Especially after hearing how vicious they were. He should have, after seeing the unicorn.

"Oh dear God," Lincoln said. "What kind of sick, twisted human being would make them look like this. Look at them."

"I am," Macy replied.

The line of goblins stood there, they were unarmed. Their small squared off feet held up their tiny, nearly naked bodies with a slight pot belly and no gender identity at all. Their heads were huge, almost too big for their bodies, and as described, they had crazy hair. A lot of it, it stuck straight in the air in a point and varied in color from goblin to goblins. Purple, pink, orange and green. Their faces, for lack of a better word to Lincoln, were kind of adorable. Big oval eyes, shiny with no pupils and a wide closed mouth smile.

They were lined up, and they moved, but only turning left and right, like they were stuck in a glitch.

"What is wrong with them?" Macy asked.

"I think Ted and Ignatius must have arrived. The Maniacal Master has them on pause."

"What do we do?"

Basa walked up to her. "There is no choice. We must slay them."

"Slay them, but … but … they look so harmless and nice," Macy said.

"Do not let their cute and cuddly nature deceive you. They are horrendous murderous monsters that will eat your heart after they take it. Now, if you'll excuse me."

"Basa," Macy called to her.

Basa fired up her swords.

"I can't let you …"

Basa didn't hear her, she raced to the line of goblins.

Macy jumped and cringed, turning away, when the first fiery sword went through the midsection of the first troll.

<><><><>

There was TV in the corner and a couch. But Harold Neemo sat in a chair before a long table desk.

On the desk was two monitors. One had a sequence of numbers and letters continuously scrolling, and on the other monitor was a game.

The corner of his desk had used paper plates, and empty juice boxes and energy drink cans were scattered everywhere.

Harold looked almost exactly as Ted had pictured him. A man of about thirty, a touch overweight, messy brown hair, and wire rim glasses. He wore a white dress shirt and tie as if he were going to attend a video meeting, but unseen, he wore a pair of green sweat shorts.

"I don't know you guys, I don't know why you're here. But leave, okay?" Harold told them. "I'm busy."

"We're not leaving until you stop playing that game," Ted told him.

"I'm not gonna stop the game. Especially since this is the first chance I had to get back on in hours," Harold said. "I've been running around for …" he raised his voice. "My mom! Bank, post office." He lifted the remote. "I know Dick Harris in Accounting has already submitted his game. That bastard. So, I have to finish mine."

Ignatius looked up at Ted and gave a nod.

"Harold!" his mom called just as her footsteps were heard on the stairs. "Honey, I made you a ham and cheese sandwich." She brought down a plate and a juice box. She set it down, then lifted the dirty one. "Would your friends like a sandwich?"

"They aren't my friends," Harold said.

"Oh, honey be nice." She faced Ted and Ignatius. "Do you want a sandwich?"

"No, thank you," Ted said.

"I'll have one," Ignatius said.

"Juice box or energy drink?" she asked.

"Juice box please."

"Be right back." She took a step, paused, looked at Ignatius and shook her head. "I can't believe how much you remind me of an old friend."

Ted waited until she walked up the stairs and moved toward Harold. "Look, Harold, about this game."

197

"I can't talk right now. I need to finish ..." He lifted the controller and faced the monitor. "What!" he blasted. "What happened to my trolls! They're all dead! Son of a gun. These adventurers took advantage of the pause. Asshole. Bet one of them is Dick from accounting. He's probably mad I killed the Prince."

"You didn't kill the Prince," Ted said.

"Yeah, I did."

"No, you didn't. The unicorn only bit off his arm. They saved him," Ted said.

Harold scoffed. "You don't know what you're talking about ... wait. how do you know that?"

"Because this game..." Ted pointed to the monitor. "It's real."

"No shit, I'm playing it," Harold said.

"No, dude, it's real. Have you not paid attention to the news?" Ted asked. "Haven't you seen what's happening?"

"Um, no, I've been playing this game nonstop. I need that hundred grand. I want out of this town.

"Wait." Ignatius pointed to the monitor and one of the players. "Is that supposed to be me?"

"What?" Harold snipped. "No, I'm not poking fun of height-challenged people, that's a fairy. And it's just standing there because the guy playing isn't using him."

"That's because I'm here," Ignatius said.

"What are you talking about?" Harold asked.

Ted explained. "This game. You dropped a link at the end of *Wind and War* to funnel players to your *Dragons of Aberly* game. You did it to get someone to play the game."

"Okay, yeah, I did. It didn't hurt anyone."

"It killed a million people!" Ted blasted. "This is real. You believed in this game so long, it manifested and is real. When I clicked on the enter button to your game, it opened a portal merging your game, dragons and all, with our reality."

"No way. How can I do that?" Harold said.

Ted growled. "The ability of the fairy is what?"

"Manifestation," Harold answered.

"You are part fairy, so you have that ability."

"Cool. Wait. No." Harold shook his head. "Fairies aren't real. My mom made that up,"

Ted nodded at Ignatius. "Show him."

Ignatius slid off his jacket and turned his back to Harold, flapping his wings.

With an, 'Uh' Harold shrieked.

"If you don't believe us about the destruction and dragons," Ted said, "Ask your mom. She's watching it on the news."

Harold jumped from his chair. With a running thump-thump-thump-thump, he raced up the stairs. His foots steps stopped above them, he shrieked again and ran back down, plopping in his chair.

"Oh my God, oh my God, oh my God," Harold grabbed Ted's hand. "I didn't mean any of this. I didn't. I swear. I was just excited someone clicked on the link to play. I thought I had some players in my game. I didn't know everything I did was actually happening."

"It is," Ted said with relief.

"I just set up a massive attack against the remaining players, killer baby dragons and all."

"I know," Ted repeated. "Which is why it has to stop."

"If I pull the plug, shut down the game, the dragons aren't going to go anywhere. They'll still be here," Harold said.

"Can you create another portal?" Ignatius asked.

"I didn't create the first one," Harold said with a panic. "I only created another level to another world."

Ted shook his head. "It's not going to work, there is only one way to stop this all. End it for good."

"Okay. Okay." Harold nodded. "Whatever it is, tell me, I'll do it."

"Cool," Ted replied. "You just have to put in a game-ending quest."

Harold froze. "Come again?"

"Game-ending quest. You have to end the game."

"End? End the game? A game I designed, I created, you want me to destroy it?"

"Yes."

"No!" Harold said. "It's not gonna happen. I'm not going to end this game. I worked too hard on it. If I collapse it, then I am out of the running for the money. I need to show them it's a great game. There has to be another way. To make the game just a game."

"How!" blasted Ted. "You've manifested it so that our planet is now the game."

"Is that right?" A cunning look came over Harold. "What does that make me then? … your friends will just have to play on and beat the next wave."

"No! It's not right and it's not possible. They don't have the ability, the power, the health or weapons to beat what you set up."

"Not my problem."

"Yes, it is!"

"No, it's not, and I won't stop this. I suggest you make the most of your powers." He dramatically sniffed. "This isn't about a hundred grand any more. This is about being God." He put on his headphones, grabbed the remote and turned to the monitor. "There is nothing you can do or say about it that will make me change my mind."

"Wanna bet?" Ted marched up the stairs.

NINETEEN

FINAL RESOLVE

"I can't believe you told my mom." Harold sulked in his gaming chair.

"It was drastic Dude," Ted said. "I know, but I did what I had to do."

His mother scolded, "Harold Ignatius Neemo…"

"Uh!" Ignatius screamed.

"What?" asked the mother.

"You called him Ignatius," Ignatius replied.

"It's his father's name."

"Uh!"

"Stop," Ted told him.

"Okay." Ignatius paused then his eyes widened, 'Oh."

"Oh, what?"

Ignatius shifted his eyes to Harold's mom. "Oh."

It hit Ted and his eyes also widened in revelation. "Oh."

Harold's mom gave Ignatius a little pinch. "I knew you'd remember."

Ignatius smiled nervously.

"But this first," she said. "Harold," his mother spoke firm. "This game has been your life. I get it. I do. But I have told you, time and time again, you have an ability to make things happen and look. Look what happened."

"Maybe … maybe it's a coincidence," Harold said.

"Stop," she said. "Was it a coincidence that you wanted to go to prom, couldn't, watched the movie Carrie and the gym burned down?"

"Oh, dude," Ted said.

"It was faulty wiring," Harold defended.

"Didn't I tell you that you caused the presidential election results?"

"I thought you meant, every vote counts," Harold said.

"Harold, gosh darn it!" she scolded. "I will change the Wi-Fi password and not tell you what it is. I will hide the keys to my car and cancel Netflix if you do not do what needs to be done. Now."

"But mom …"

"Now!" she blasted.

"Fine."

"Thank you," she huffed, inhaled folded her arms and turned. "I'll get that sandwich for you." She walked back upstairs, paused and glanced back. "And Iggy. Let's catch up." She winked.

After his mother had left, Harold swiveled back and forth in his chair, tapping his hand on the desk. "I hate losing all this work. Years of it."

"I get it," Ted said. "I do."

"To be honest I don't know how to get things back to normal," Harold said.

"None of us do."

"No, I mean, I don't know how. I never planned on the game ending."

Ignatius asked. "Can you just not add a reward to the current quest? Freeze the mobs and let the team go and slaughter the dragons, crush the eggs and the rest."

"Oh, that's cold. Those eggs are babies," Harold replied. "And no. It's not that simple with the dragons. The goblins, unicorns, I put the game on pause, they pause. The dragons are more complex, they are AI-driven. I don't control their offensive moves; I control what they do with them. Does it make sense? Like, they'll attack, I just say what they attack: city, town, or village. When the quest players battle them, I only control how they fight back. If I quit or don't do anything, it's not like the goblins, the dragons will still be going strong."

"Almost as bad as just shutting things down," Ted said.

"Not quite that bad, so what do I do?" Harold asked, then looked thoughtful. "I can add the separation of worlds as a quest result. And I can supply the players with better weapons."

"That could work," Ted said. "Plus, they have the United States Army fighting with them."

"Um …" Harold stammered. "Conventional weapons will work on the four that are there, but the three new red ones, I created a buff. Bullets don't work on them."

"Can I kill this guy?" Ignatius asked. "When it's all said and done, can I kill him?"

"No," Ted replied. "He didn't know he was doing it for real. And well, you're his father."

Ignatius shrieked.

"Dad?" Harold asked with a cracking voice.

"No!" Ignatius blasted. "Well… probably."

"Stop," Ted told them.

Harold tossed up his hands. "Guess you'll have to call the quest team or whoever remains and tell them they'll just have to fight as best as they can. Because I'm at a loss."

"No, you're just not trying. We have to come up with something."

Ignatius glanced to Ted. "Think, my friend. Think. You are the Thinker."

Harold baulked. "I didn't create a thinker."

"No, you didn't. We did," Ignatius replied.

Ted's eyes lit up. "I got it. Create a nerf."

Ignatius looked confused. "What is a nerf."

"See that screen," Ted pointed to the other monitor. "That's the development code for the game. In games where players find an exploit to make themselves overpowered, the developers step in with what we call a nerf to create a weakness. They rewrite the code for the magic weapon or whatever it is that is too powerful." Ted looked at Harold. "Can you do that? Nerf the dragons?"

"I … I can't touch their AI, but yes." Harold turned to the other monitor and put his hands on the keys. "I can think of a couple of ways I can nerf them."

"Make it something fun," Ted told him. "Creative."

"Got it," Harold said. "It will take me a couple hours."

"Even better. It's getting dark, nothing will happen, and it will give us a chance to get back and be a part of it." Ted had a sudden thought. "And while you are at it. Boost my Charisma to max will you?"

Harold's hands clicked away on the keyboard. He stopped. "You guys aren't turning me in to the police or anything are you?"

"Let's see how this thing plays out," Ted said. "Get it … Plays out?"

Ignatius groaned. "I'll ignore that bad pun. Let's get back. Good luck, Harold."

"Thanks, Dad."

Ignatius grumbled. As he turned for the stairs with Ted, Harold's mother stood there.

"Are you leaving?" she asked. "I made you a sandwich."

"We have a flight, but if you don't mind," Ignatius said. "I'll take it with me."

"Absolutely." She handed him the paper plate and the juice box. "Be safe."

"Thank you," Ted replied and looked back at Harold frantically typing, "I believe now we will be."

<> <> <> <>

Lincoln couldn't get the vision from his mind. In fact, he was certain he never would. That vison would cause nightmares for the rest of his life. Every time he would sleep or close his eyes, Lincoln knew he would see it.

It was horrible.

It wasn't supposed to be, but it was.

Even as he stood on that first crest of the mountain, staring at the seven dragons that circled in formation high in the night sky above the dragon eggs that now glowed and wriggled.

Deep in the threat of immediate annihilation, he couldn't stop seeing the massacre brought on by Basa.

Basa was proud of what she had done, and even took a bow afterwards.

Tiny troll limbs were scattered about everywhere. Even the green blood didn't take away from the brutality Basa showed toward them. No mercy. Lincoln just couldn't fathom how they were dangerous. They looked like toys.

He would have to take Basa's word for it, that it was like with the bunnies.

Basa was poised and ready, standing alongside at least thirty armed US soldiers ready to fire upon the dragons when they were closer.

The sound of slurping, a straw sucking up the last few drops, caused Lincoln to take his eyes from the sky and peer down to Ignatius.

Ignatius sucked on the tiny straw of the drink box. "Sorry, these things are really good."

"You don't seem concerned," Lincoln said.

"I'm not."

"My friend," Samuelson said. "Your brother assured us it was handled. Did you not, Ted?"

"I did. We're good. He nerfed them," Ted said.

"Does that ..." Lincoln pointed to the dragons. "Look like they are weakened? No. They are like vultures, waiting to attack. We have spotlights here, Ted, they can see us."

"That's fine. We're ready if they attack. I just talked to Harold on the field phone," Ted told him. "He says all is good."

"There are seven of them," Lincoln replied. "I'm sorry. But I don't trust this. They never fly at night, yet there they are."

"All part of Harold's plan," Ted replied. "Look, we can't end this until we face off. If we wait until morning, they're going to hit another city or somewhere. There are seven. The only way to do this final battle is to do it now, draw them to us. Make them come to us."

"Okay, brother, I hope you're right," Lincoln said. "You know Ted, you've really changed. There's a star quality about you these days."

"I know, dude, wanna compare our Charisma scores?"

"Wait," Lincoln, "you didn't?"

"I call the win."

Macy inched her way to the brothers. "We're ready," she said. "On your call."

After a smirk at his brother, Ted raised his rifle. "Give the command."

Macy nodded. "Sergeant Mitchel. Fire a calling shot."

Doug lifted his rifle and fired a single shot into the air.

That shot brought about a sudden change in the flight pattern of the dragons. They formed a V, the largest dragon was center, with three dragons flying behind it on both sides.

"Everyone ready!" Doug called out. "Give it all you got when they're close enough."

"Basa," Ted called her. "You have to go for the red ones. Bullets won't kill them."

Basa raised then fired up her swords. "I am ready."

The lead dragon flew like a torpedo downward. It cried out loud and screeching in attack mode. Almost in range, it lifted its body, arched back its neck and widened its mouth. There was no doubt, it was ready to blast those below.

When the dragon brought its head forward, mouth aiming at everyone on the ground, he released his physical rage. Instead of a roar blasting fire, happily little musical notes played as a rainbow stream of steam poured from its mouth.

Lincoln saw that and heard the heavy patter on the ground that sounded like hail. He peered down to see teeth. Dragon teeth.

"What the hell?" Lincoln asked, his weapon lowering in his shock. "Rainbows and no fire. Did they all just lose their teeth?

"Yes, they did, big brother, yes they did. Now raise your rife. This is it," Ted said. "Game over."

TWENTY

POST GAME SHOW

Ten Months Later

Slayer, Sally and Don

The end of the reign of the dragons was cause for celebration but better still were the quest rewards. When the last dragon dropped to the ground, the night turned into day and with a strong wind a carpet of color rolled over the tristate region and magically, buildings sprang back up out of the dust, like a film running in reverse, everything was restored. Even though it seemed to be a complete reset, the return home hadn't erased what had happened from the minds of those who witnessed it.

In the aftermath, it was like a mental exhaustion plague broke out. Businesses shut down; people needed a break.

The president and congress immediately released a Dragon Initiative and Stimulus package for those effected by the dragon attack.

For the first time in twenty years, Ted, Lincoln and their mom weren't neighbors with Aunt Sally and Uncle Bob. Those two opted to use their stimulus money for a move to Las Vegas.

Sally got a job at a salon, and Bob worked the door as security at a famous brothel. Both of them saying they would be happy never to see another wooded area or dragon again.

They had already been planning their way to dryer, deader land when the final battle took place. They stayed in a camp until their home suddenly reappeared. Then packed up and left.

Once the dragons had been rendered toothless and fireless, they had been easy to kill. Their awkwardness and strength still caused some injuries, but Basa was able to slay five out of the seven herself. Garnishing paise and newspaper headlines, not to mention the multitudes of television interviews, Slayer rose to quick fame, helped by the fact that she was amazingly beautiful as well.

When they dragons fell, they unfortunately destroyed most of the eggs they landed on. All but three were crushed.

With permission from the United States Government, Basa asked to study the eggs and train the dragons when they hatched. She believed they could be trained and she was right.

Her showmanship and Shakespearean manner of speaking gained her not only notoriety but a one-woman show called Basalous the Slayer and Her Magical Draconem Friends. She'd tell Slayer tales of the past and bring out the smaller-than-average dragons to dance and perform tricks. The highlight of the show was when the dragons blasted the audience with a rainbow-colored, thick steam, allowing the audience to leave not only happy but with a fruity scent to them as well.

She was so popular her shows were sold out. Fortunately for her, but unfortunately for Sally and Bob, Basa landed a two-year residency show in Vegas.

Sally and Bob were happy to see Basa again and have her around, the dragons on the other hand, were a different story.

The Son, the Mom, the Prince and the Wizard

The core Williams family didn't want to be separated, after all that had gone down with the dragons. So Lincoln, Ted and Bea waited until Lincoln's company could transfer him. It took only a couple weeks, and they moved the entire family, along with Paxton, Sam, and Ignatius to Newcastle, a suburb of Seattle, Washington.

It was the first time in a long time that the three of them each had their own place, Bea struggled for a while with whether she wanted to go back to hairdressing. She had bills to pay. She ended up getting a job at a nursing home as their beautician. It was rewarding and lunch, while not always tasty, was free. Plus, she had to work, even though Paxton helped with paying the rent, things were tight. At first, she felt bad for the all-knowing Sam. He put together an income piecemeal by penning opinion articles and blogs for hire. He'd dictate them and Bea would type them up. Sam struggled the most at adapting in his new world. His citizenship hadn't come through, and even though the government gave him a temporary visa so he could work, it was tough getting a job.

No one was hiring a wizard with no experience, especially one that claimed to be two hundred and six years old, no matter how much he looked like Sam Elliott. Then finally, when he was visiting Bea at the nursing home, a production company was filming a commercial and hired Sam on sight: he ended up being the Sam Elliott lookalike spokesman for Happy Haven Retirement Living.

Other than the incredible strength he acquired, the slight new drinking problem, the urge to tattoo his entire body while searching for three breasted women, Lincoln's life was pretty much the same.

And Lincoln kept the perks of being the stand in Barbarian.

Life was good.

His apartment was similar to the one he had in Pittsburgh. And the three restaurants he managed looked exactly like his previous Arby's, except they had espresso machines and an open mic poetry reading on Fridays.

His new crew was friendly and he was able to get his Pittsburgh Assistant Manager a transfer to his store as well. It was slightly busier than his old Arby's but the customers were laid back. Lincoln liked it. He tried to be a hands-on manager, which made him different to the other GMs that had been there before.

Even new jobs had the same old issues, like the sandwich maker dropping the buns behind the toaster. Lincoln had just pulled out the counter when he noticed a missed call from his mom.

He immediately called her back, because she only usually texted.

"Mom? Everything okay?"

"Yeah, oh, yeah, I was on my way to you, something came in the mail. I'm in the lot."

"Come on in, we aren't busy," Lincoln said. "Must be important. Is it for me?"

"No. It's for him. I know he's working. I believe it's good news."

"Excellent," Lincoln said, "I have good news to give him, too. So I think you should be there. Is Sam with you."

"Now, you know he's not. It's almost three," Bea said.

Lincoln groaned. "Oh, I forgot. Come in." He hung up the phone and waited by the fryer until he saw her.

Envelope in hand, Bea walked into Arby's and to the counter.

Paxton was behind the counter, a male customer was ahead of her, and she waited. He turned around and smiled brightly. "Welcome to Arby's how can I help you, today."

"Wow," the customer said, "You have truly awesome hair."

"Thank you. What can I get for you?" he asked.

"I'll take one of everything on the menu. Especially if you're serving."

Paxton smiled and rung up the customer. After the transaction was finished, Bea walked up to him.

"Bea!" he said with delight.

"You just look so handsome in your uniform."

"Thank you," Paxton lifted his head proudly.

"And the way those sleeves fall, you don't even notice the prosthetic."

"I am working magic with it. Are you hungry?"

"I ate at work, but I brought you something." She handed him an envelope. "It's from the Department of Immigration."

"Oh! My hands are shaking. I can not open it, can you?"

Bea giggled. "Okay." Excitedly she ripped the envelope open and pulled out the paper. Her eyes skimmed. "Oh! Paxton, your final hearing is next Tuesday, you become a citizen."

"Did I just hear that correctly?" Lincoln said as he approached. "He's becoming a citizen officially?"

"Yep." Bea nodded.

"This is great." Lincoln walked from behind the counter to the door. A bell was there that customers rang when they had great service. Lincoln rang that bell several times. "Can I have your attention everyone. Our fine employee, Paxton Prince will not only be an official American Citizen on Tuesday, today he was named Employee of the Month."

The customers and employees applauded.

"For exemplary service, dedication." Lincoln said. "Defining 'service with a smile' and increasing sales by two thousand percent." He walked every and handed a plaque to Paxton. "Take a look. That and your picture goes on the wall of pride."

Paxton held the plaque, then glanced to the wall with employee photos. "This is such an honor, thank you my general manager friend."

"You are very welcome. You're a good employee." Lincoln patted him on the back.

"See? See?" Bea said. "You may not be wielding a mighty sword, but everything about you is still enchanting."

"You are too kind and sweet but make no mistake my fine yellow haired friend." Paxton smiled. "One day, even with a single arm, I will wield a mighty sword again."

The Genius in the Basement

Harold Neemo didn't go to jail, for that he was grateful. No one truly believed he intentionally set out to burn three states to the ground, but nevertheless, even though everything had returned to normal, he was ordered to serve one thousand hours of community service which he did by teaching computers to senior citizens in the next county.

He didn't mind it, not at all. Harold was still able to build websites for people, do coding for apps, but he was forbidden for a period of ten years to create any more video or computer games. That irritated him. He had created what he believed was the greatest game ever, and not only did he lose the hundred grand to Dick from Accounting, he lost his job at the game company.

He was able to make a living doing side jobs. As far as making another game went, Harold lived and breathed *Dragons of Aberly*, there was never another game in the back of his mind. He envisioned it could become as famous as *Dungeons and Dragons.* And so it had, but not in the way Harold wanted it to be.

A lot of things changed about Harold. Since the community service, he wasn't strapped to the computer all the time. He even thought about joining a gym, but he was taking the health thing one day at a time. He also had been texting Ignatius regularly, trying to make a connection there. In fact, Harold was all about making people connections.

Having signed up for a dating site, Harold was currently anxious to see if his profile had any hits. He rushed home from his community service, stopping at the store for his mother and at a takeout place for subs. He even bought one for her.

He put the bags in the kitchen: his mother could unload them, he was in a rush to get to his office.

"Aw, Harold this is so nice," his mom said. "You got me a sandwich."

"I did."

"Are you eating with me?"

"If you don't mind, I want to go downstairs, see if I got any hits."

She held up her fingers. "Fingers crossed."

Grabbing a juice box, and carrying his sandwich, Harold went down to his basement office.

He placed his sandwich on his desk, and opened the wrapper, spreading it out like a plate. After undoing the tiny straw, he placed it in the beverage.

The moment it popped the seal, his computer started to beep. A steady beep, like an alarm.

Slowly, he swiveled his chair to face the monitor.

In a bold, white 1980s Atari style lettering with a black background, the words, 'Ready Player One' flashed over and over on the screen. Under them it read, "Maniacal Master an opponent awaits.'

The 'click to play' button seemed to scream at Harold and all he could do was stare.

The Thinker and The Wizard

It was a new life for Ted, one that he absolutely loved. A fresh start in more ways than one. He never dreamed the West Coast could be for him. But it was.

He and Ignatius gained a small bit of fame for being the influence behind stopping the dragon attacks. They both hit the news circuits for the first month. Even Ted's ex-wife called and asked him to take her back. To which, he replied, "Um … no."

That small bit of fame helped Ted and Ignatius start their own business. Each day it seemed more successful. They made a good bit of money from what they called honest work and helping others at a discount price.

They were partners in a life coach program called, 'Thinkers and Doers', where they had the uncanny ability to figure out people's problems and solve them by helping them get what they want.

They offered a money back guarantee. No one ever asked for a refund.

"That's great," Ted said on the speaker phone in the car. "Tell him we'll take him to dinner."

Ignatius nodded. "Anywhere he wants to go."

"I'll tell him. If he got the papers, so did you Ig," Lincoln said.

"We're on our way home," Ted told him. "We'll see then. Hey, we picked up a new client today. We got another great review."

"You guys suck," Lincoln told him. "Try really making an honest living instead of exploiting that Charisma buff."

"We are."

"No, Ted, using your abilities is cheating."

"I beg to differ. Talk to you later bro." Ted waited until his brother hung up and he ended the call.

"Unbelievable," Ignatius said, staring at his smart phone.

"What? Harold texting you again?"

"Yeah, but I kind of owe him a fishing trip or something. Harold doesn't bother me," Ignatius said.

"Then what is it?"

"Basalous was spotted again with that Leo actor guy. Man, he is too old for her. And … and the Kardashian Jenners keep reposting her tweets."

"Quit being jealous."

"I'm not, she's just always …" Ignatius grumbled. "What does she see in humans?"

"Same thing I do. What do you find attractive?"

"Fairy women."

"Well, good luck with that."

"I'll find one. You watch."

"It doesn't count if you Manifest one." Ted pulled into the driveway. "Home."

"Thank God. Let's hurry." Ignatius opened the car door and jumped out at the same time as Ted.

They both raced up the walkway and into the house.

"Uh!" Ted shrieked when he saw Samuelson sitting on the couch staring at the blank television. "Why haven't you started?"

"I can not figure out this darn thing." Samuelson held up the remote. "It's still on your game machine."

"Oh, my bad. I have to change the mode." Ted took the remote.

"It's probably still on the news network," Ignatius said. "I was watching the debates."

Ted switched the television to cable mode, and when he did, the news was on. Just as he was about to change the channel, Ignatius reached up and stopped him.

"Look," Ignatius said.

On the screen was a bad home video, it was shaky. It showed a mountain range, clouded sky, and the target image was slightly pixelated from being enlarged.

At the bottom of the screen, the ticker banner read, 'Cloaked skeletal man spotted flying over mountains in the Southeast Asian country of Laos. Experts say image is fake.'

"Ted?" Ignatius asked.

"You don't think…?" Samuelson asked.

"Nope." Ted switched the channel. "Nope. You know what that was, it was footage from *He Man* or something. Someone is pulling a hoax."

"Are you sure?" Ignatius asked.

"Positive. Someone would have had to have clicked on that link at the end of *Wind and War*. Harold got rid of it." Ted plopped down. "I … think."

"You think!" Ignatius blasted.

"Yeah, I'm sure, well, pretty sure, I mean, how could he forget to do that? Right? It's a biggie. Now stop. There are no more fantasy games invading our world. But there is …" Ted upped the volume. "*The Secret Storm.*"

Ted didn't worry about it, nor did he want to worry about it. To him, the odds of a gamer apocalypse happening again were impossible. It was time to relax and watch their show. It was their daily ritual. Life was good and safe. Ted wanted it to stay that way.

Just as his show started to play, he groaned when a loud, pounding knock game at the door. "Seriously?"

Annoyed, Ted stood and walked to the front door. He pulled it with a fury, blasting out an angry sounding, "What!" as the door opened.

"Friend!" Arms wide, Barbarian stood there smiling. "I am back." He stepped inside. "It is good to see you." Bruce grasped Ted's arms, giving him a greeting shake that nearly jolted him from his stance. "I am ready to slay whatever beast dares to cross our path! Oh, is that *Secret Storm*?" He slipped by Ted, walking to the living room.

Ted stood there, still holding the open door. Greeting cheers from Ignatius and Samuelson came flowed from the living room.

The dragon, unicorns, bunnies and all of that other stuff may have gone, never to return again. But after seeing Bruce and the image on the television, in Ted's mind, it was far from being … game over.

ABOUT THE AUTHOR

Jacqueline Druga is a native of Pittsburgh, PA. Her works include genres of all types but she favors post-apocalypse and apocalypse writing.

For updates on new releases you can find the author on:

Facebook: @jacquelinedruga

Twitter: @gojake

www.jacquelinedruga.com

Level Up publishing specializes in LitRPG and GameLit books. If you have enjoyed *Apocalypse: Dragons!*, you might be interested in our other titles, which can be found at: www.levelup.pub/books

To join our mailing list for news about forthcoming books and opportunities to be an ARC reader, just fill in the form on that page.

You can also find us on:

Facebook @LUPublishing

Twitter @LevelUpPub

www.ingramcontent.com/pod-product-compliance
Lightning Source LLC
Chambersburg PA
CBHW020106180626
46812CB00006B/2497